Promise You Won't Tell?

John Locke
Writing as Dani Ripper

TELEMACHUS PRESS

This book is a work of fiction. Names, characters, places and incidents are either the product of the author's imagination or are used fictitiously. Any resemblance to actual persons, living or dead, or to actual events or locales is entirely coincidental.

Promise You Won't Tell?

Cover Designed by: Telemachus Press, LLC
Copyright © Shutterstock/118832569

Visit the author's website:
http://www.donovancreed.com
http://daniripper.wordpress.com

Published by: Telemachus Press, LLC
http://www.telemachuspress.com

ISBN: 978-1-939337-23-8 (eBook)
ISBN: 978-1-939337-24-5 (EPUB)
ISBN: 978-1-939337-25-2 (Paperback)

Printed in the United States of America
10 9 8 7 6 5 4 3 2 1

Promise You

Won't Tell?

Chapter 1

Monday.

**"I saw you on TV this morning promoting your business,"
Jana Bagger says, entering my office.**

"Great! How did I come across?"

"Like stink on a turd."

"Wow! Thank you!"

She gives me an odd look.

I extend my hand, she takes it. It feels odd, somehow, two women shaking hands.

Jana sits. "Should I call you Dani or Ms. Ripper?"

"Dani's fine."

"You're young."

"I'm twenty-four."

"As I said," she sniffs.

"Being young has its advantages, Jana."

"Such as?"

"I've got boundless energy!"

"That's it?"

"I'm enthusiastic."

"Same thing."

"I've got perky breasts."

She glances at my chest and sniffs again, unimpressed. Then says, "I wasn't aware you had valet parking, Ms. Ripper."

"Please, call me Dani. Regarding the valet parking, we're very service-oriented when it comes to our clients."

"Am I a client, then?"

"Yes. We've agreed to take your case."

"I drive a terribly expensive car. I'm not sure I trust my M6 to that scruffy teenager out front."

"His name's Dillon. He's a good driver."

"How well do you know him?"

"Quite well. Why do you ask?"

She hesitates. "I don't want to get him fired. He might follow me home and burst my skull like a ripe mellon."

"Dillon almost never does that to new clients. You can speak freely."

"He was eating from a box of cereal when I pulled up."

"Dillon likes his sugar."

"His hands were sticky. I made him wash before touching my car keys."

"Always a good idea," I say.

We're quiet a minute. Finally she says, "How much do you charge?"

"A thousand to take your case, five hundred a day to work it. If we haven't solved your case in four weeks, we work for free till we do."

"That sounds terribly expensive."

"Not after the fourth week."

"I doubt you'll work very hard after the fourth week."

"You're right. We probably won't work on your case at all after the fourth week."

"What, you just give up?"

I shrug.

She frowns. "That doesn't inspire much confidence."

"We only take cases we can solve quickly. If we give up, we offer a complete refund, minus the initial thousand for taking the case."

"Theoretically, you could take a thousand cases, solve none of them, and pocket a million dollars."

"Yes, but our references would be non-existent."

"So you have references?"

I shrug. "No. But it's not because we're failing to solve cases."

"Your response begs explanation."

"It does?"

"If you don't mind."

I pause a moment, thinking up an example. Then say, "If we prove your husband's cheating, you'll be upset, right?"

Jana says nothing, so I add, "Upset clients don't give written recommendations."

"Perhaps they're upset for other reasons."

I frown. "We can probably get some wives to tell you we caught their husbands having affairs."

"You keep saying 'we.' Do you have other employees?"

"Partners."

"Can I meet them?"

"No."

"I beg your pardon?"

"They're highly skilled, highly connected, highly placed. Diligent, but low profile. I'm contractually obligated to protect their identities."

"You make it sound as though your partners are in the CIA."

"Yes, absolutely."

She arches an eyebrow. "Your partners are in the CIA?"

"No. But I agree it sounds that way."

She frowns. "You fancy yourself witty."

"Witty, with enormous breasts. But that's my fancy. Truth is, they're just perky."

Jana's expression says I'm failing to win her over, but we both know she needs me. She clears her throat and says, "As I mentioned last week in our phone conversation, I think my husband's cheating on me."

"And you wanted us to find out."

"Yes."

"And you thought he might be seeing his new secretary, Darcie Darden."

"Not *seeing* her. *Fucking* her."

"I understand the difference."

"That's encouraging. How long will it take you to find out?"

"In dollars, twenty-five hundred."

"That's..." I wait for her to do the math. "Three days? You think you can catch my husband cheating in the space of three days?"

"Yes."

"That seems ambitious."

I open my desk drawer, pull out a file, lay it on the desk, and tap it with my fingertip.

"We already have," I say.

"Have what?"

"Solved the case."

"What are you talking about?"

"Whenever possible, we like to solve our cases before accepting them."

"That's preposterous."

"Maybe so. But it helps our success rate."

"You've got proof in that file?"

"Yes."

"May I see it?"

I open the file and remove the top sheet, the application.

"I'll show you everything. After you fill out the paperwork and pay the fee."

"Son of a *bitch!*" Jana screams.

"It's just paperwork," I say.

"Not *that*, you nitwit. My husband."

"What about him?"

"You've obviously caught him cheating. You couldn't prove in three days he's *not* cheating."

"That's very astute," I say, handing her a pen.

She starts crying.

I'd attempt to comfort her, but she appears to like me less than a baboon likes diaper rash. Plus, my cell phone picks this very moment to chirp a text message. It's my secretary, Fanny, claiming to be sick.

As usual.

I text back, *I don't believe you.*

5

The office phone rings.

"Dani Ripper, private detective." I say, cheerfully.

"Ms. Ripper, it's an honor. My name's Eric Cobblestone. Are you still taking cases?"

"I am. Do you have one for me?"

"I think my wife is cheating on me."

"I expect she is."

"Excuse me?"

"In my experience, if you think your wife is cheating, you're probably right."

He pauses a moment. Then says what they all say.

"I...I need to know for certain."

And I say what I always say.

"Of course you do."

"How do we proceed?"

I look to see if Jana is filling out her paperwork.

She is.

"Ms. Ripper?" Eric says.

"Yes?"

"How do I become a client?"

"I'll need a thousand dollars and a pair of your wife's panties."

Jana looks up at me. I motion her to continue filling out the form.

"Excuse me?" Cobblestone says. "Did you say you need my wife's panties?"

"Yes. What's her name?"

"Erica."

"You're joking."

"What do you mean?" he says.

"Your name's Eric, hers is Erica?"

"That's right."

"That must get confusing."

"Why?"

I let it go. "Is Erica still sleeping with you?"

"Not so much these days."

"Can you talk her into it?"

"Probably...Possibly...Maybe...No, probably not. Why do you ask?"

"Get her to have sex with you. Then pay attention to the panties she puts on afterward. When she removes them, put them in a plastic bag and bring them to me."

"Her soiled panties?"

"Yes, of course."

"Why?"

"Because I'm a degenerate."

Jana looks up. I motion her to continue.

"I'm kidding," I say to Mr. Cobblestone. "It's part of the process."

"The kidding?"

"The panties."

"So you're serious?"

"About the panties? Yes, absolutely. Let me know when you've bagged them."

"Can I ask what you intend to do with them?"

"I'm going to test them in my lab."

"Test them for what?"

"Don't make me say it."

He pauses. "Semen?"

"Ugh. Yes."

"But..." he seems exasperated. "You'll only be proving *I* slept with my wife."

"That's correct."

"This conversation makes no sense!"

"See? That's why I hate taking cases over the phone."

"This conversation would be less confusing in person?"

"Just get the panties. Then call for an appointment. Trust me, I'll find your wife's lover."

We hang up. Before I have a chance to deal with Jana, I get another text from Fanny.

I've never been this sick in my whole life. It's possible I'm dying.

I text back, *Prove it. In person.*

Fanny texts, *I'm serious. These might be my last words.*

I text back, *Your last words to me will be "You can't fire me."* *But I will.*

Jana pushes the completed form across my desk. I give it a quick review.

"Did you bring your checkbook?" I ask.

She sighs, writes the check, pushes it across the desk. I pick it up, make sure it's properly dated and signed, and place it in the slot on the wall behind my chair.

Then I open the folder, show her the evidence.

"The first page shows your husband's driving history. The two entries that count are highlighted in yellow. This one's the Colony Motel, on Brookwood. Ever been there?"

She shakes her head no.

"Tuesday at noon your husband entered the motel lobby, took the elevator to the third floor, knocked on the door of room three-fifteen. The door opened, he entered. Fifty-one minutes later, he exited the room. Thirty minutes after that, a

8

woman exited the room, took the elevator down to the lobby, and checked out."

"Was it Darcie Darden?"

I show her a photo.

Her face turns crimson, then bursts into flames. Well, not literally, but trust me when I tell you she's pissed.

Cover-your-ears pissed.

"Home-wrecking *cocksucker!*"

I pause to make sure she's referring to Ms. Darden, and not me. Then say, "Our operative followed Ms. Darden to fourteen twenty-six Riverside, which happens to be the second highlighted trip your husband made."

"When?"

"Eight o'clock this morning."

She looks at her watch. "You mean he's there right now?"

"Possibly."

I show her a photo of the house and ask, "Recognize it?"

"No. But that can't be Darcie's house."

"Why not?"

"Look at it."

I do, but I don't understand.

"What's wrong with it?" I ask.

"She's my husband's secretary."

"So?"

"This house is nicer than *mine!*"

"I agree it's nicer. But why can't it be hers?"

"Is it?"

"No."

She smiles as if she's won a victory, but a hollow one. Like a tennis player who wins a match when her opponent double-faults the final serve. But the idea she's smiling after hearing the house isn't Darcie's, confuses me greatly. Maybe it's because I don't play tennis.

She interrupts my thoughts by asking, "Whose house is it?"

I sigh. "This is what I hate about my job."

"What are you talking about?"

"The house belongs to your husband."

"*What?*"

I nod.

"Max has another house?"

"Yes. And this is it."

"He's *renting* it?"

"No."

"He—you can't mean he *owns* it?"

"Yes."

She stares at the photo.

It really *is* a nice house.

She says, "My husband, Max Bagger, owns this house."

"That's correct."

"And Darcie Darden lives there?"

"She appears to."

Jana starts crying again. I put my hand on hers. She recoils in horror. "Are you *hitting* on me?"

"Excuse me?"

"It's a simple question," she says, regaining her composure. "I asked if you were hitting on me."

"No, of *course* not!" I say, defensively. Then ask, "Why would you think that?"

Why indeed? She's not even Max's first choice.
She says, "It's a well-known fact you're a lesbian."
"It's a...*what?*"
I sigh.

Chapter 2

Do I really need to explain my sexual orientation to Jana Bagger?

And if so, what would I say? Would I tell her I kissed a girl? And liked it?

I *could* say that, because I *did* kiss a girl.

My best friend, Sophie Alexander. In a limousine last month.

And I *did* like it.

To be completely truthful, I kissed her a lot.

Yup, pressed the button on the arm rest and waited till the privacy panel was completely up. Then Sofe and I fooled around on the back seat for more than an hour.

What do I mean by "fooled around?"

We...you know. *Did* a few things.

To each other.

You know, with clothes on.

And without.

It was all very experimental.

I mean, I knew what I'd *find* under Sophie's clothes, it's just that I wasn't sure what I'd *do* when I found it.

When I found *them*, I mean. You know...the different things I uncovered.

Under her clothes.

Anyway, I wasn't sure what to do, so I took a cue from Sophie, who seemed to know *exactly* what to do with what she found under *my* clothes.

And then I sort of—you know—did the same things to her.

Which was pretty much...everything.

As far as I know.

...And I liked it.

But...we haven't done those things since, even though we live together.

Nor have we talked about it.

Maybe it's a limo thing.

Maybe it's something else.

In other words, I'm still confused.

It's...

It's a long story. Even Jana doesn't want to hear it. If she did, she wouldn't be changing the subject.

She says, "My husband Max owns another house?"

"Yes. A very nice one."

"For how long?"

"According to the deed, three-and-a-half years."

"That doesn't make sense. Darcie's only worked for him a few months."

"Four months next week," I say.

"Do you have proof he fucked her on Tuesday?"

"No."

"Maybe he had another reason to meet her at the Colony Motel."

"Maybe they were planning a surprise party for you!"

She scowls. "Don't be flippant. Although a surprise party makes more sense than your claim they were fucking in a motel room."

"How so?" I ask, noting the frequency with which she drops the "F" bomb.

"If he's putting her up in a house, why not fuck her there?"

"Probably because of her mother."

"What about her mother?"

"She lives there."

"Darcie's mother lives in Max's house?"

"Yes."

"Max won't even let my mother *visit* us!"

"I think she lives there because of the child."

"*What* child?"

I sigh. "I should probably find another way to earn a living."

"*What* child?" she repeats.

"William Darden. Willie."

"Excuse me?"

"Darcie's son. The one she had with Max."

"*What?* Oh my *God!*" she yells.

She stares straight ahead, processing the information. I take the opportunity to remove the video disk from her file and cue it on my laptop. I press play, and angle the screen so she can see the video of Max knocking on the motel room door, and entering, then leaving, then getting on the elevator. Then Darcie leaving the room, returning the key to the front desk, getting into her car, and driving to Max's other house.

Jana's crying.

"Things will be okay," I say.

"How can you possibly say that?" she snaps.

"I can't. I was deliberately trying to comfort you."

My cell phone vibrates with Fanny's latest message.

Can't...breathe. Coughing up blood. Oh, God!

I text back, *You're not fooling anyone. Get your ass to work or I'll fire you!*

Jana says, "I can't end our marriage without positive proof."

"I have copies of the deed and birth certificate."

"Positive proof they're fucking."

I pause a moment, then ask, "Are you aware how often you use the "F" word?"

"For five hundred a day I'll say *fuck* as often as I please!"

I make a note to put a no-cursing clause in my next contract. I mean, I like fucking as much as the next girl, but I don't feel the need to *say* the word. Not constantly, anyway. And I certainly wouldn't feel the need to say it just because I paid a fee for an unrelated service. I can't imagine visiting my banker and saying *fuck* all the time just because I'm making mortgage payments.

Having said that, now that I think about how much interest I paid last year compared to principal, I *do* feel fucked.

Two years ago—before he died—my husband Ben talked me into watching a porn flick. Within five minutes a couple was doing it, and she kept yelling, "Fuck me! *Fuck* me! Oh, my God, FUCK me!"

I pressed the pause button and Ben groaned, "You're already disgusted?"

"Confused," I said.

"About what?"

"She keeps telling him to fuck her."

"So?"

"What does she think he's *doing*, if not fucking her? I mean, what did she think he'd say, *No, I'm just going to keep doing this for a while, and maybe I'll fuck you later?*"

Ben said, "Jeez, Dani, it's porn, not Fellini."

"What's Fellini?" I said.

Poor Ben. I never really loved him, but we made a pretty good life together. Until I was accused of murdering him. As it turned out, someone else murdered him. But that didn't have a positive impact on our relationship, either.

"What if I get you a video of them having intercourse?" I ask Jana.

"How would you do that?"

"I have people."

"Your partners?"

"Highly skilled, highly trained, highly connected."

"How long will that take?"

"We'll have to wait for the next motel visit. Are you prepared to pay our daily fee till that happens?"

"Can I get some sort of discount?"
"No. But after the fourth week—"
"It's free?"
"Exactly."

Chapter 3

"**Did you get her check cashed?**"

"Yes," Dillon says, and hands me a stack of fifties. I peel five from the pile and put them in his sticky hand.

"You've got to stop eating those Sugar Smacks. They make your hands sticky."

"That's not from the Sugar Smacks."

"*Omigod!*" I say, jumping back, staring at his hands as if they held live snakes.

"What's wrong?" he says. A devilish look crosses his face, and he suddenly becomes the boy you always tried to avoid on the playground at recess. He makes his hands into claws, holds them up, and comes at me.

I back up. "*Omigod!* Don't *even!*"

He stops, confused.

"That's the most disgusting thing I've ever heard!" I say.

"What're you *talking* about?" he says, staring at his sticky hands. Then his face turns red. "Oh, shit. You don't actually think—"

I shake my head. "Let's drop it. I don't want to know."

"I can explain."

"Trust me. I don't want to hear!"

"It's paste."

"I don't care what you call it. You can't just go around *doing* that!"

"Jesus, Dani. Seriously, it's paste. We use it to seal the envelopes, remember?"

"Not really."

"Remember last month when we ordered ten thousand envelopes in bulk and they showed up with no glue on the flaps?"

"Vaguely."

"I called the company to complain and they said glue costs extra, and requires an extra step during the ordering process?"

It's all coming back to me like a bad dream. "I thought you sent them back for a refund."

"They refused them, and shipped them back. And charged us extra shipping. And a processing fee."

"Why did we deal with this ridiculous company in the first place?"

"They gave me a great price."

I frown.

Dillon says, "It's not a big deal. I only mail a hundred lead letters a day."

"Are you listening to yourself?"

"What?"

"You're a computer genius, Dillon. A *genius*! Which is why I made you a full partner in the business."

"I know. And I'm very grateful. I've got a car now, an apartment, and—"

"And you're pasting envelopes."

"So?"

"That's Fanny's job."

"Fanny's sick."

I frown. "How long have we had this office?"

"About a month."

"In all that time, why haven't I met Fanny?"

"She's been ill."

"Have you, in fact, ever met Fanny in person?"

"Yes, of course. We talk all the time."

"You speak to her."

"Yes."

"She speaks back."

"Of course."

"You're referring to actual words."

"Yes."

"Spoken by a human voice? Not texted or simulated?"

He nods.

"How did you happen to find Fanny in the first place?"

"She was working for one of our vendors."

"Which one?"

"The envelope company."

"The same envelope company that sold us ten thousand envelopes with no glue?"

He nods.

"Let me guess. Big boobs?"

He shrugs.

"Great. Note to self. Don't let teenage boys pick out the receptionist. Dillon?"

"Yeah?"

"Tell her to get her ass to work."

"Okay. But I think you're being kind of hard on her."

"Of course you do."

He says, "Till she gets here, someone has to do the mailings. I can't help it if I suck at pasting."

"If that's really paste all over your hands, the letters you sent must be even stickier."

"Cool idea," he says, changing the subject.

"Which idea is that?"

"Installing the slot behind your desk so the clients' checks fall into my office. That way I can run to the bank and cash their checks while they're still talking to you about their cases."

"Did you wire Jana's car?"

"Of course. As always."

Another of my "cool" ideas, as Dillon would say. Pretending he's the valet parking guy instead of my partner. After parking the clients' cars he installs a tracking device in the trunks of their cars.

"Dani?"

21

"Yes?"

"Sorry about the envelopes."

I look at him. Dillon's eighteen, with runaway acne and long hair he keeps in a ponytail and neglects to wash. He's six-three, and so skinny my mom would say there's more meat on a butcher's apron.

If Mom was still alive.

Though socially inept, Dillon truly is a computer genius. He's incredibly talented with anything electronic. Toss him some nuts and bolts, give him an hour, he'll build you a lunar space module.

Apart from his computer skills, he's a work in progress.

And sensitive.

I smile to let him know I'm not upset about the envelopes.

"Wash your hands, okay?"

"Okay."

I go back to my office, sit at my desk, think about how dull my job is. I'm a private investigator, but virtually all my income is derived from decoy work. Wives pay me to see if their husbands are cheaters. Fiancés pay me to test the integrity of prospective husbands. Attorneys pay me to test the fidelity of clients' spouses. Campaign managers pay me to test their opponents' characters.

I keep trying to move beyond decoy work. It's not an admirable profession. Decoys are two clicks below hookers, and only six above politicians.

But the truth is I'm good at it.

How good?

Two weeks ago a deadly assassin paid me a hundred thousand dollars to see if I could seduce his girlfriend.

Why so much?

In his line of work love's a luxury. His girlfriend, also an assassin, had been living a lesbian lifestyle for years. He had to be absolutely convinced she was ready to hang up her dildo.

It was a thrilling assignment, dealing with volatile people who kill at the drop of a hat (which may explain why you don't see many people wearing hats these days). Flirting with this assassin, *playing* her, was exhilarating. But the investigative work I've been doing the past two weeks?

Boring.

Half the time I'm at my computer, digging through records. The other half I'm in my car, or Dillon's, waiting for something to happen. And by that I mean—brace yourself—a man or woman might walk out of a house or hotel room!

Together!

Yawn.

Not long ago I was consumed by a real case. A serial killer was on the loose, one who preyed on teenage girls. Having been abducted by a similar killer/rapist at an early age, I devoted countless hours to solving the case.

But the payoff?

Zero.

Monetarily speaking.

The P.I. sign makes the phone ring, but decoy work pays the bills.

People don't realize it, but decoy work requires incredible skill. You need to be a psychologist, great listener, great conversationalist. A wardrobe master, great dancer, an enthusiastic, effective flirt. A tease. You must also be sensual, cute, adorable, cunning, clever, and so much more.

By comparison, being a P.I. requires a computer, a car, and a reliable bladder.

I hate routine investigative work! And the clients? Don't get me started! My current book of clients would tax the patience of a sloth. No proctologist in the country sees more assholes each week than me.

In general, I mean, because every now and then you strike gold. You get a real client with real problems and you get a shining opportunity to feel good about your job.

My passion is helping victimized kids.

I can relate to them.

I understand them.

They trust me.

Don't get me wrong: I don't sit around hoping kids will be victimized just to keep me from getting bored. But when bad things *do* happen, I want to be the one who gets the case. I'll work night and day for them, put everything else on the back burner. I...

I look up at the young lady who just walked into my office.

A teenager.

"Ms. Ripper?" she says.

"Yes?"

"I'm Riley Freeman. Umm..." She looks around a minute. I notice her fingers fussing with the hem of her pleated skirt.

She's nervous. Confused about something. This could be it. The case I've been hoping for.

I stand.

"Hi, Riley."

I come around my desk, shake her hand.

"I don't have much money," she says.

"Who does?" I say. "Please. Have a seat."

She looks around, uneasy.

I motion to one of the chairs in front of my desk. "Please," I say.

She takes one, I take the other.

"How can I help you?"

"I only need a minute," she says.

But the way she says it tells me this is going to be huge.

Chapter 4

"I think something might have happened at the party."

"What party?"

"Well, it wasn't exactly a party," Riley says. "Not at first. It started out as a sleepover."

I study my potential client. She's cute, in a blonde, surfer, little sister sort of way. Her hair's parted in the middle, and falls over narrow shoulders. She's thin, willowy, with smallish breasts, perfect teeth, and wide-set amber eyes.

I love amber eyes. Did you know they're the fourth rarest of all colors in human eyes? I know weird things like that. I also know amber eyes are the most common color among wolves' eyes.

I remove a pen and legal pad from my desk drawer and say, "When was the sleepover?"

"Last Saturday night."

"Who's house?"

"Kelli Underhill."

"Were her parents there?"

"Her mom."

"Who was invited?"

"Four girls were invited. Me, Jennie Cox, Cammi Churra, and Parker Page. Parker's my best friend. She left at midnight."

"Any boys?"

She bites the corner of her lip. Then says, "Some boys came by later."

"How old were they?"

"High school juniors and seniors."

"Seventeen?"

She nods.

"Were any of them eighteen?"

"I don't think so."

"And you're what, seventeen?"

"Yes, ma'am."

"Did you know these boys?"

"They go to my school. Carson Collegiate."

"You said something might have happened at the sleepover Saturday night."

"Yes, ma'am."

"Tell me."

Chapter 5

"We were playing Truth or Dare," Riley says.

"...And one of the dares was to steal a fifth of vodka from the liquor cabinet."

"And you did?"

"Cammi got the dare."

"All the girls drank?"

"Yes, ma'am."

"Did Kelli's mom know about the drinking?"

"No. She wouldn't have allowed that."

"Can I assume you drank too much?"

She nods.

"When did the boys show up?"

"Just before I passed out."

"Tell me about that."

She sets her jaw bravely, and says, "I felt sick to my stomach, so I went upstairs to Kelli's bedroom. She's got her own bathroom. I was dizzy, and thought I might need to throw up. When I came out of the bathroom, I sat on Kelli's bed, then passed out."

"Was the bedroom light on or off?"

"On."

"You're sure?"

"Yes, ma'am. I turned it on when I went in the room."

"Did you close the door behind you?"

"Yes, ma'am."

"You're positive?"

"Yes, ma'am. Like I said, I thought I was going to be sick. I was embarrassed. I didn't want anyone to hear me throw up."

"How long were you in the bathroom?"

"I don't remember. A few minutes, I think."

"Then you went to the bed and passed out?"

"Yes, ma'am."

"Any idea what time that happened?"

"A little before midnight."

"How do you know?"

"Because Parker's mom picked her up at midnight. But she was still in the basement when I went up to Kelli's room."

"And Mrs. Underhill was asleep at the time?"

"I guess so."

"Where's her bedroom?"

"On the main floor. But she was sleeping in the guest bedroom."

"And where is that located?"

"On the other end of the hall from Kelli's bedroom."

"How far away is that in feet?"

"I'm not sure."

"Do the Underhills have a big house?"

"Huge."

"How many bedrooms upstairs?"

"Four, I think."

"More than one staircase?"

"They've got two. I used the back one, and came up from the basement."

"So Mrs. Underhill didn't hear you come up the stairs?"

"No, ma'am."

"You're sure?"

"If she'd heard me, she would've come out of her room to ask why I was upstairs. We were supposed to stay in the den or the basement the entire time."

"Where were the girls going to sleep?"

"In the basement. They've got six beds down there."

"So when did you wake up?"

"The next morning, around nine."

"How'd you feel?"

"First thing I did was throw up in the bathroom. I had a terrible headache all day."

"Did you feel groggy? Like you might have been drugged?"

"No ma'am. Just however you'd feel after being drunk all night."

"So you woke up in Kelli's bedroom, and threw up. Then what happened?"

"I heard the girls downstairs, in the kitchen, making breakfast. So I went down."

"How'd they react?"

"They were shocked to see me. They thought I'd gone home with Parker."

"And you told them what happened?"

She nods.

"What did they say?"

"They said they got wasted, too. But they slept in the basement."

"And they never came up to Kelli's room the whole night?"

"No, ma'am."

"Does that seem normal to you?"

"Normally, they probably would have gone to Kelli's room at some point during the night. We usually did that."

"But not this time? You're sure?"

"Yes, ma'am. I asked them about it."

"What did they say?"

"They didn't want to get caught. They were afraid Lydia—Mrs. Underhill—would find out they'd been drinking."

"Makes sense," I say.

I take a minute to think about everything she said. Then ask the big question.

"Tell me about the boys."

Chapter 6

**"There were ten guys in two cars. One of them texted Kelli
and said they were in the driveway."**

"What time was that?"

"Around eleven-thirty, I think. Something like that."

"And Mrs. Underhill was upstairs in the guest bedroom
with the door closed?"

"Yes ma'am. She might have been asleep, or watching
TV."

"Who let the boys in the house?"

"Kelli."

"And her mom never knew?"

"I don't think so."

"They just happened to show up at the right time?"

"Ma'am?"

Her constant use of the word "ma'am" is driving me
crazy. I'm twenty-four years old. Young enough to be her sister.

Would you call your sister "ma'am?" Should your slightly-older sister call you "child?"

I ask, "Was it just a coincidence they showed up at Kelli's soon after her mom went to bed?"

"No ma'am. They'd been exchanging text messages with Kelli all night."

"Did the boys know you were there?"

She thinks a minute. Then says, "I'm not sure."

"Did they see you?"

She studies the Galileo thermometer on my desk for a minute. It's a sealed glass cylinder filled with liquid. Inside are five multi-colored floats that rise or fall depending on the room temperature.

"I like this piece," she says.

"Thanks."

She points to the lowest float above the halfway mark. "Does this mean it's seventy-two in here?"

I nod.

She says, "We were in the basement, drinking. When the guys showed up, the girls jumped up and ran to let them in. I jumped up too, but felt like I was going to throw up. So I went up the back stairs."

"No one came looking for you?"

She shakes her head no.

"Why not?"

"I think they all sort of forgot about me when the boys showed up."

"And you didn't wake up till the next morning?"

"No ma'am."

"What were you wearing?"

"Pajamas."

"Bra and panties underneath?"

"Panties. No bra."

"Did the pajama top have buttons? Or was it a pull-over?"

"Pull-over."

She looks at the thermometer some more.

I say, "What do you think happened to you that night?"

"I think I was molested."

"By whom?"

Riley's eyes are suddenly full of tears. A couple spill down her cheeks. She dabs at them with her hand.

"I'm not positive anything happened," she says. "Or who might have done it. It could have been one person, or..."

Her voice trails off.

"Or what?"

"Everyone."

"The girls *and* boys? You think it's possible your girlfriends would let that happen to you?"

"No. It's just that...I have no idea who might be involved. I'm just saying I can't rule anyone out. If something happened, it was probably one boy. Or maybe two. Because the girls wouldn't have let all those boys roam around the house by themselves."

"But one or two boys might have snuck up the back steps?"

She nods.

"Tell me what you mean by 'molested.'"

"They might have...you know, *touched* me. Inappropriately."

She starts shaking, and her tears start flowing, as if saying the words was all it took to open the floodgates. I reach across the desk and put my hand on hers. When she looks up at me I say, "Do you have any reason to suspect you were sexually assaulted?"

"You mean..."

"Any evidence you were penetrated?"

Her eyes go wide. "No, ma'am!"

"But you think you were touched? Groped?"

She pauses. Then says, "Not just that."

I look at her. "What else?"

"I'm pretty sure someone undressed me, too."

Chapter 7

I hand her a tissue and wait till she stops crying.

After she composes herself I say, "When you woke up, were your clothes on?"

She nods.

"Then why do you think someone undressed you?"

"At school today, Rick Hooper said something. Right out-of-the-blue."

"Was Rick at the house that night?"

"No, ma'am. He's a nerd."

I frown. "Why would you say that?"

"I just meant that Rick wouldn't have been invited to ride around town with the cool guys."

"What did Rick say to you at school today, out-of-the-blue?"

"He gave me this sly sort of grin and said, 'I heard you passed out at the sleepover, Strawberry.'"

"Is that your nickname?"

"No."

"I don't understand."

"You know how some people have tattoos on their lower back, like one of those fancy script things, with maybe a heart in the middle?"

I nod, wondering where she's taking me with this conversation.

She says, "I always wondered what it would look like to have one. Of course, my mom would *never* go for that! So anyway, when I was in my closet getting dressed to go to the sleepover I noticed an old sticker book from when I was a kid. I peeled off a little sticker of a strawberry, and put it...you know, down there."

"Under your panties?"

She looks down at her hands, and I notice her ears and neck turning red. And her cheeks.

"Yes, ma'am. I was hoping to find something bigger I could stick on my lower back, just to—you know, look at it? Just for fun? I'd look at it in the mirror, then throw it away. But all I had in the sticker book was the little strawberry, so I put it in a private place in the front. I looked at it and thought it looked kind of cool, but then the doorbell rang, and I threw my clothes back on and forgot all about it."

"This happened the night of the sleepover?"

She nods.

"While you were still at your house?"

"Yes, ma'am."

"Who rang your door bell?"

"Parker. Her mom gave me a ride to Kelli's house."

"Did you tell Parker about the strawberry sticker?"

"No."

"Why not?"

"For one thing, I forgot all about it when Parker showed up. But even if I *had* remembered, I'd be too embarrassed to talk about it."

"Why? You're best friends. It's sort of funny."

"What if she *told* someone? I'd be mortified!"

"Why?"

"Seriously, Ms. Ripper? A *strawberry?*"

I shrug. "I've seen worse."

She gives me a look of concern.

I say, "Parker's mom picked her up from Kelli's around midnight?"

"Yes, ma'am."

"Any reason she might not want Parker spending the night at Kelli's house?"

"Parker had church the next morning. Her mom didn't want her up all night."

"Who took you home Sunday morning?"

"My mom."

"Did you say anything to her about what might have happened?"

"I didn't know anything might have happened till yesterday at school, when Rick Hooper called me Strawberry. But I wouldn't have said anything to my mom anyway. That would be too weird."

"So she didn't know you were drinking, or that Kelli let boys in the house."

"No ma'am."

"Did you and Parker talk about what happened that night?"

38

"She said everyone went back down to the basement to hang out and drink. Parker figured I was in the bathroom. When her mom called to say she was on the way, Parker told everyone goodbye, and went upstairs to check on me."

"Did she find you?"

"No ma'am. She checked the rooms and bathrooms on the main floor, but didn't have time to go upstairs because by then her mom showed up."

"Did you tell Parker what Rick Hooper said?"

"Not yet."

"Why not?"

"Parker's my best friend. If I told her what happened, she'd flip out and start accusing people. By tomorrow, the whole school would be talking about it."

"So you came to me, hoping I could conduct a secret investigation?"

"Can you?"

"No."

"How about a quiet one?"

"Probably not. But I can try."

"How much would it cost?"

I smile. "How much do you have?"

"Four hundred dollars."

I give her a look.

She says, "Four hundred and twenty-seven dollars, to be exact. This is money I saved from babysitting, birthdays, and Christmas cash. I've earned a lot more through odd-jobs and part-time work, but last year I started a charitable foundation, so I put the rest of my money into that."

I say, "Riley, I can't take your case."

Her face falls.

She says, "I could pay you more, over time."

"It's not the money. It's the fact you're a minor. I can't enter into a contract with you without your parents' permission."

"I don't have a father. And I can't tell my mom yet. She'll freak. And what if I'm wrong? I'd be getting her all worked up for nothing."

I sigh.

"Is there anything you can do?" she asks. "Without involving my mother?"

I think about it. "I suppose I can ask around, see what I can find out."

Her face lights up.

"I'd be asking as a friend of the family, not officially."

"Okay."

"But there's something you need to know, Riley."

She looks at me. "What?"

"People talk."

"What do you mean?"

"Whether something happened or not, everyone I talk to will tell someone else. What I'm saying, we won't be able to keep a lid on this. And if something actually *did* happen, you'll want to file criminal charges."

"This wouldn't go to trial, would it? Since they're all juveniles?"

"More likely, some sort of hearing. But a judge would preside, and both sides would have attorneys."

"We don't have much money, Ms. Ripper. I suppose the court would appoint an attorney to represent me."

"If things get to that point, I might be able to help you."

She says, "I chose you because of what happened to you when you were my age."

I was two years younger, actually, but who's counting?

She says, "And I've read about how you spent all these years trying to help other kids."

I nod.

She pauses, then says, "I'm not gay."

"Excuse me?"

"I just didn't want there to be any misunderstandings. You know, about you helping me for free?"

I frown.

"I'm not gay," I say.

"You're not?"

One hour in the back of a limo last month, and the whole world's talking about it? What's going on here? Did someone stick a note on my forehead today?

Actually, I know how this whole "Dani's gay" rumor got started.

I'm high profile.

I'm not bragging or anything, it's just a statement of fact. I'm known as *The Little Girl Who Got Away*. The story of how I was abducted by a serial killer/rapist gripped the nation nine years ago. Sure, I changed my name, started a new life, but my identity became public just before Ben was murdered. As the wife, I became the prime suspect. It was a media circus. The world "found" me hiding out in Sophie's house, here in Nashville. Sophie's popular in her own right. She's a well-known songwriter, and locally, a well-known country singer.

She's also the niece of Salvatore Bonadello, who happens to be crime boss of the entire mid-western United States.

It's quite common for young women to live together without being considered lesbians, but Sal has a huge extended family, and Sophie "came out" a few years back. Naturally, the word spread like wildfire that his niece, Sophie, had a new girlfriend.

Who happened to be famous.

Not that you're asking, but Sophie and I did nothing sexual the first month we lived together. Of course, one might argue the main reason for that is my husband Ben had just been murdered.

It felt too soon for sex.

But later, like I said, we did it.

Once.

And I liked it.

But I'm still in-between deciding if this is what I really want. It's not Sophie's fault I haven't worked it all out yet. She's been great. My problem is the bastard who kidnapped me really screwed me up, psychologically.

Riley says, "What happens now?"

"I need to have a chat with Rick Hooper."

"Oh, God," she says.

"What?"

"It's starting, isn't it?"

"It is. Where can I find him after school tomorrow?"

"You mean, where can you talk to him privately?" She thinks a minute, then says, "He works at a movie theater, part-time."

"Perfect."

Chapter 8

Tuesday.

It's a tricky business, interrogating a minor.

Rick Hooper's the afternoon manager at Skyline Theater, Chesterfield Mall. It's not much of a job. Not at three-thirty on a Wednesday afternoon, at least.

I wait till the third and final customer gets his popcorn and soft drink, then motion from across the lobby for Rick to join me.

This is the point where I need to explain that I'm good-looking, and hope I can do it in a way that doesn't sound offensive. By way of example, in the past two months I've placed top ten among the world's most beautiful women in two national magazines. And although it's a tragic symptom of the type of media we have in this country, there's a reason the entire nation was fixated on my kidnapping nine years ago, and on my sudden re-appearance earlier this year.

Young women disappear every day, right?

But they only make a fuss over the ones the media considers pretty.

It's not right, but it's true. You know it and I know it. And I'm ashamed that my abduction was front-page news, and received daily TV coverage, when so many other girls might have been saved had the media simply shown their pictures and told their stories one flipping time.

But they didn't.

I don't take any credit for my looks, just as you wouldn't take credit for having wonderful parents, or being born brilliant. These are lucky accidents of nature.

I'll understand if you think I'm conceited. But if I'm allowed to say this without sounding cocky, there aren't many seventeen-year-old boys who wouldn't cross the floor of a movie lobby to talk to me when I motion to them to come over.

And Rick Hooper is no exception.

"Can I help you?" he says.

"Are you Rick Hooper?"

"Yes."

"We need to talk."

"About what?"

His eyes suddenly grow big. "Omigod! You're Dani Ripper!"

See what I mean? I'm not saying everyone recognizes me, but I'm reasonably well-known.

"Please, keep your voice down, Rick. I'm here for a reason. A serious one."

He goes from excited to nervous. His brow furrows.

"What's wrong?"

"The bad news is you may be involved in a serious crime."

"*What? Me?*"

"The good news is I'm in a position to help you."

He looks around. "Is this a joke? Am I being filmed?"

"It's no joke. And you're not being filmed. But you *are* being recorded."

I show him my cell phone.

"You're a private investigator."

"Yes."

"I don't know anything about a crime."

"This tape and my testimony will be proof that you're cooperating. For what it's worth, I believe you had nothing to do with it."

"With what?"

"Riley Freeman."

The look on his face tells me I caught him completely off-guard. His brain's going a thousand miles an hour trying to comprehend where I'm going with this. Finally he says, "What about her?"

"Are you and Riley close friends?"

"No. I barely know her. I mean, everyone knows Riley. She's popular. But..."

"But *you're* not?"

He laughs. "Do I look like one of the cool kids to you?"

"Yesterday at school you called her a name."

"What are you talking about?"

"You called her Strawberry."

The color drains from his face. "No I didn't!"

"Lying could get you a felony charge. You called her Strawberry," I repeat.

He looks at my phone, then into my eyes. His expression tells me it's true.

"Who told you?"

"Riley Freeman."

"Look, I'm not sure what she thinks she heard, but I never said that."

"You did, Rick. And I need to know why."

His lip quivers. He tries to speak, but his voice breaks. He clears his throat. Then says, "I'm not saying anything without an attorney."

I click my phone to stop the recording.

"You don't need an attorney, Rick. Not yet, anyway. But you will if this case goes to the police."

"I haven't done anything wrong!" he says.

"If the police get involved they may accuse you of obstructing justice."

"Why?"

"Because on Sunday or Monday, someone told you what happened to Riley Freeman at Kelli Underhill's slumber party."

"Not true."

"The police will expect an honest answer."

"If the police ask me about it, I'll demand an attorney."

"I can save you the time, trouble, and expense, and make sure the police know you cooperated from the start."

"No way. I'm not saying anything."

"Look, Rick. I know you had nothing to do with it. You weren't even there. But you know something."

"It's not that big a deal."

"You're wrong. It's huge. A serious crime has taken place. Think about it from Riley's perspective."

I pause a moment, hoping he will. Then I say, "You remember when you were a kid in school, and the teachers said if you did something wrong it would go on your permanent record, and follow you the rest of your life?"

"They still say that."

"Seriously? At your age? Well, I can promise you, it's bullshit."

"I'm not sure I understand your point."

"Police reports are different. They're the ultimate permanent record. What do you think the detectives will put in the police report when they investigate Riley's case? They're going to say the investigation was launched because of a comment made by Rick Hooper."

His face goes from pale to paste.

"I-I can't talk about this," he says.

I touch his arm, look into his eyes. "Rick, you're a good guy. I'm almost certain you are. And maybe you think Riley's a stuck-up bitch, and maybe there's a part of you that's happy this happened to her, because maybe it's nice to see a popular girl getting knocked off her pedestal for once. Or maybe you want to protect the person or people who told you what happened Saturday night, because they're the cool kids, and you were impressed they confided in you."

"No one confided in me. They don't give a shit about me."

"You overheard it?"

He looks around.

I don't know if he's making sure no one's listening, or hoping someone in the lobby might require his attention. In any event, the lobby's dead, and no one's going to rescue him.

He says, "I might have heard someone talking about it on a cell phone. But that's all I'm going to say."

I frown. "That's not enough, Rick. I need to know what was said."

"I'm sorry, but it's not my job to tell you. I'm not *like* you, Ms. Ripper. I'm an outcast. A social misfit. I just want to get from one day to the next. You caught me by surprise a minute ago, but you can't prove I know anything. If the police ask me, I'll tell them I never called her Strawberry, and never overheard anything. It'll be your word against mine, and I'll have an attorney with me. No one can prove I overheard him talking about Riley Freeman. No one!"

"Him?"

His face flushes. "I'm not saying anything else."

He turns to leave.

"Rick?"

"What?"

"I know you wish you hadn't spoken to Riley yesterday, but you did. And you can't take it back."

"You can't prove I called her Strawberry, and she can't prove it either."

"You already admitted it to me."

He smiles. "Not on tape."

I reach into my jeans pocket and remove my other cell phone, touch a couple of buttons, and play back what he just said.

His face flushes. Now I can't nickname him Casper.

I put the phone back in my pocket and say, "It's just a matter of time, Rick. The fact you overheard something proves it's being talked about. When this blows up it's going to be huge. It'll be on the evening news and the front page of the paper."

"So?"

"Right now, guess how many names Riley can give the police? One. Yours. Do you really want the police to have *your* name, instead of the guys who actually *did* something? Do you want them to start this investigation by coming to *your* house, talking to *your* parents?"

His lips twitch again. In a very small voice, he says, "Can you keep my name out of it?"

"Probably not. But I *can* make sure the police know you cooperated fully. And I can guarantee you won't get in trouble over it."

"This totally blows," he says, practically in tears. "If only I'd kept my mouth shut."

"You couldn't. You wanted Riley to think you knew her secret. It gave you power over her."

"You make me sound pathetic."

"I was in high school once upon a time."

He frowns. "Don't even try to tell me you weren't the most popular girl in school. Head cheerleader, homecoming queen, the girl every guy dreamed of having."

49

"I might've been all those things," I say. "Except that a rapist named Colin Tyler Hicks kidnapped me, beat the shit out of me, stole my innocence, locked me in his fucking basement, and—"

"I'm sorry," he says. "Please don't cry."

What?

Am I crying?

Shit.

He gives me a hug.

I cry some more.

"I'm sorry," I say.

"It's all right. It's my fault."

I pull away and say, "I feel like an idiot."

He smiles. Then says, "Welcome to my world. To tell you the truth, I'm surprised Riley even knows my name."

"Go figure," I say.

"What did she say about me?"

"Honestly?"

He nods.

"She called you a nerd."

He laughs.

I laugh.

"Please, Rick. I know she might not be the most thoughtful person in the world, and maybe she's had it a bit too easy in life, and maybe she's treated you badly in the past. But she's a human being. And only seventeen. And the victim of a crime. Peer pressure got to her. She screwed up and drank too much. But what happened to her isn't right. It's not fair. And it's not her fault."

He sighs.

"Give me a name," I say.

He sighs again, looks around, then whispers, "Ethan Clark."

"Close your eyes, Rick."

"Why?"

"Just do it."

He does.

I give him a quick kiss and say, "You're one of the good ones. I'll make sure Riley knows you came through for her."

He opens his eyes. "You think there's any chance in the world that..."

"What?"

"You think I'd ever have a chance with Riley?"

I shrug. "Who knows, right? Stranger things have happened."

"What's your honest opinion?"

"Not in a million years."

We laugh.

"Story of my life," he says. Then adds, "Why is that, do you suppose?"

"Are you asking why girls like Riley aren't interested in guys like you?"

"Yeah."

"What's your favorite food?"

"Cheeseburgers."

"Riley likes broccoli."

"Ugh."

"There you go."

I start to leave, then turn and say, "One last thing."

He rolls his eyes. "What now?"

"Did Ethan have personal knowledge of what happened, or was he repeating the story?"

Rick closes his eyes, shakes his head as if he can't believe this is happening. "I'd rather not say."

"Then don't. Just nod if he had personal knowledge of what happened to Riley Saturday night."

I wait.

He nods.

"Thanks, Rick."

"Please. Keep me out of it."

"I'll do my best. Will you tell me what you overheard?"

"No."

I give him my card and say, "We're friends now. If you change your mind, call me, okay?"

He nods.

As I walk away he says, "Thanks."

I turn. "For what?"

He shows me a sheepish grin. "That was my first kiss."

Could that be true? I study him a moment.

It can.

"I'm honored," I say.

Chapter 9

At five o'clock I unlock the front door of my office, look at the vacant reception desk, yell "Damn it!" and text Fanny.

Where are you?

Hospital.

Oh yeah? Which hospital? Which room?

Sorry, ER nurse just told me to turn off my cell phone.

The front door opens and a very red-faced Eric Cobblestone enters, holding a paper bag at arms' length.

He takes a seat across from me, places the bag on the desk.

"Your wife's panties?" I say.

He nods. "They're in the plastic bag inside."

"Congratulations!"

"I beg your pardon?"

"You weren't sure she'd have sex with you."

"It wasn't easy, I can tell you that."

I believe him.

"Well," I say, "That part's behind us. Your determination is about to pay off."

"I hope so, because this is the most embarrassing thing I've ever done in my life."

"It is? Seriously? Why?"

"Are you kidding me? That's fluid from my body. You're going to be *looking* at it. *Inspecting* it."

I say, "Have you never given a doctor a urine sample?"

"Not on a pair of my wife's panties."

"Good point. Still, I can't help but think you're making too much out of this."

I peek in the bag.

He says, "What happens next?"

"We apply a chemical to the stains."

"To what purpose?"

"The stains will turn a specific color based on the unique protein compounds in your semen."

"Like a fingerprint?"

"Exactly."

"And how will that help us?"

"We'll compare it to the backflow in her panties next week."

"What do you mean?"

"Next week, or whenever you suspect she's cheated on you, you'll bag the panties she was wearing, and bring them in."

"And?"

"I'll test them. If they contain semen, it'll show up a different color than yours."

"What if she's sleeping with my identical twin brother?"

"Do you have an identical twin brother?"

"Not that I know of, unless we were separated at birth."

"Well, in that absurdly ridiculous case, the stains would probably be the same color."

"So it's not so unique after all."

"I suppose not."

"So you might not be able to prove anything. This could be a complete waste of my time."

I sigh. "If your wife is fucking any human on the planet Earth, aside from a non-existent identical twin brother, the stain will be unique, and easily distinguishable from yours. Can you trust me on this?"

He shrugs. "What choice do I have? I can't continue carrying this paper bag around with me wherever I go. Today a co-worker asked if he could share my lunch."

"Well, her panties are safe with me. And we'll get to the bottom of them."

"What's that supposed to mean?"

"It means we'll soon have our answer."

He says, "Is there some sort of international semen database I don't know about?"

"What do you mean?"

"How can you tell *who* she's sleeping with based on the stains in her panties?"

"I can't. But if they contain semen stains that don't match yours, we'll know she's cheating on you. And if she is, I'll have her followed."

"If she's meeting someone, it will probably be Saturday morning."

"Why?"

"She said she has to run errands."

"Maybe *you* should follow her."

"I've got my Space Ace convention."

"Whatever that means, I'll assume you're indisposed."

"Obviously!"

We look at the bag. He says, "Can I watch?"

"Watch what?"

"The test."

"Are you serious?"

"Totally."

I sigh. *Why do I get all the crazies? Of course his wife is cheating on him. Who wouldn't?*

"Let's go," I say.

He follows me to the testing room.

"This is your *lab*?"

"I'll concede I may have overstated when I referred to it as a lab."

"It's a *kitchenette!*"

It's actually a break room, with a small table, two chairs, a refrigerator, a microwave oven, and a sink.

I say, "All I need's a place to spray the chemical. This is as good as any."

He looks around. "You *eat* in here?"

"Of course."

"Let me get this straight," he says. "You remove soiled, stained panties from plastic bags, spray them with a chemical above the sink, then sit at that table and eat your lunch?"

I frown. "Maybe not after today."

I point to one of the chairs. "Care to sit?"

"Not on your life!"

A few minutes later I show him the multi-colored hue that uniquely identifies his sperm.

"Where do you store them while waiting for the next pair?" he says.

"Uh...you don't want to know."

He follows my gaze, walks to the refrigerator, opens it, says, "I don't fucking *believe* this!"

I shrug. "Can I offer you a yogurt?"

"I'd rather have a root canal from a witch doctor."

"A simple 'no thank you' would suffice."

"After the case is closed, can I have them back?" he says.

"What, the panties?"

"Yes, of course."

"I'll insist on it," I say.

Chapter 10

"What can you tell me about Ethan Clark?"

I'm on the phone with Riley. She says, "Ethan Clark? What have you heard?"

"Rick overheard someone talking about what happened at the sleepover."

"What did he say?"

"He wouldn't give details, but Ethan's the key. Was he there Saturday night?"

"Yes. He was driving one of the cars."

"He's got a license?"

"Provisional."

"Meaning he's not supposed to drive after midnight?"

"Yes. But he does."

"What else can you tell me about him?"

"He's the richest kid in school. His parents, I mean. His dad's a corporate attorney, and married well. His wife is a Bennett."

"As in the Fortune Five Hundred Bennetts?"

"Uh huh."

"Carson Collegiate's a private school, right?"

"Yes, ma'am."

"Terribly expensive?"

She pauses, then says, "You want to know how we manage to pay the tuition?"

"It crossed my mind."

"I'm on scholarship."

"Academic? Athletic?"

"Both."

"Full tuition?"

"Yes, ma'am. They also pay for books, supplies, activities, and projects."

"You must be pretty smart."

"I was. Until Saturday night."

"There's that," I say. "What are you planning to major in, at college?"

"Criminal justice."

"Wow. You *are* smart!"

She says, "You might want to check out Ronnie English."

"Who's he?"

"Ethan's best friend."

"Was Ronnie at Kelli's?"

"Yes. Wherever Ethan goes, Ronnie follows."

"Could they have slipped away from the others?"

"You mean when they were all in the basement?"

"Yes. Could they have snuck off for ten or fifteen minutes without being missed?"

"I wouldn't think so. Unless the others were playing a game or something."

"Like Truth or Dare?"

"Or Beer Pong, or Spin the Bottle."

"Kids still play Spin the Bottle?"

"Sure. It's a classic."

"Do Ethan and Ronnie have girlfriends?"

"Ethan's dating Melanie Hughes. Ronnie's in between girlfriends, I think."

"Are they the sort of kids who'd take advantage of an unconscious girl?"

"They're the sort who'd try to drug her first."

"Have they been in trouble with the law?"

"Not that I know of. But if they have, their daddies probably paid someone off."

"Where can I find Ethan?"

"Alone?"

"Uh huh."

"I don't know. He doesn't have a job like Rick. And like I said, he's got his own car. A brand-new Mercedes, if you can imagine. But he's usually with Ronnie, or Melanie, or both."

"Must be nice to be seventeen, rich, and driving a Mercedes."

"There's something else," Riley says.

"What's that?"

"Ethan's above the law."

"No one's above the law, Riley."

"I'd like to believe that," she says, with a tone that suggests I'm naïve.

I say, "If he did something to you, we'll get him."

"I think not. But I *would* like to know."

"I'll do my best."

Chapter 11

"Is your husband home?"

"What's this about?"

I'm on the porch, talking to Kelli's mom, Lydia Underhill, who doesn't recognize me from the recent news coverage.

"How do you know my husband?" she says, letting me know she can recognize a possible marriage threat when she sees one.

"I *don't* know him. I was hoping to catch you together."

"Doing what?"

"Pardon?"

"You don't look like a salesperson. Are you campaigning for some sort of office?"

"I'd like to talk to you about your daughter, Kelli."

"What about her?"

"May I come in?"

"You expect me to just let you into my *house*? Are you *kidding* me? Who *are* you?"

"Dani Ripper."

She frowns while studying me.

"Your name sounds familiar," she says. "You *look* familiar. Where do I know you from? Carson Collegiate?"

"No. I'm a private investigator."

"Why would a private investigator be asking about my daughter?"

"It's about the sleepover Kelli had Saturday night."

"What about it?"

"After you went to bed, the girls swiped a fifth of vodka and drank it."

"Obviously, this is a joke." She looks around, then peers over my shoulder, as if expecting to find a camera crew.

"Just after midnight, two cars full of boys came over. Kelli let them in."

"Is this your idea of a joke? Because this is ridiculous! Kelli's an honor student. She simply wouldn't *do* that."

I hand her my card and say, "Talk to her about it. Then give me a call."

"Why should I?"

"Because something happened here that night, whether you want to believe it or not."

Her eyes narrow with anger. "I was here the entire evening, and remained here until each girl was safely picked up by her parent on Sunday. I don't appreciate your insinuations about my daughter, or my parenting skills. What I *would* appreciate is for you to get off my property, immediately!"

"Talk to Kelli," I say. "Then call me."

Chapter 12

Wednesday.

I follow Ethan's Mercedes as he drives his girlfriend, from place to place.

It's tough having a girlfriend sometimes, isn't it, Ethan? Cramps your style, I bet. Well, don't worry. I doubt she'll be around much longer.

Eventually, he makes his way to her house, walks her to the door, kisses her. It might have been a tender moment had he not grabbed her ass when she turned to enter the house.

Now I'm following him as he turns on Radcliff, now Wyatt, and onto the interstate. I pull up beside his car and honk my horn. He looks at me, does a double take, smiles, waves. I lower the passenger window and yell, "Follow me!"

"I'm on it!" he shouts.

Again, he's a boy, he's seventeen...you get it, right?

I pull in front of his car, take the Westport exit to Spring Valley Mall. He follows me into the parking lot. When he parks, I climb out of my car and get into his.

"You're Dani Ripper," he says. "The Little Girl Who Got Away."

"And you're Ethan Clark."

"You *know* me? How, through my father?"

"Nope."

He smiles. "You want to meet him?"

"Nope."

"Good."

We sit quietly a minute. Then he says, "If you knew how many hours I've spent trying to find naked pictures of you on the internet."

"Why?"

"Are you kidding me?"

He looks at my chest.

"I'm up here," I say.

"Sorry. I didn't mean to stare. It's just, I thought you'd have bigger boobs."

"Behave, or I'll tell Melanie."

"You know *Melanie?*"

"I know a lot about you, Ethan."

He shows me his best cheesy smile and says, "Like what?"

"Well, for one thing, I know you drive your car past midnight with a provisional license."

He grins, holds his wrists toward me and says, "Guilty as charged. Arrest me."

"You're safe. For today."

I look at his hands. "You can put them down now.

He does.

I say, "Have you been cuffed before?"

"No, of course not."

"You sure about that?"

He gives me an odd look. "I'm a nice guy. Ask anyone."

He fakes a sympathetic expression, as if to imply I hurt his feelings. Then says, "Why would you ask me that?"

"It's no big deal. Probably just a coincidence."

I can see he's curious, so I add, "You extended your hands with your palms open, inches apart, thumbs up."

"So?"

"It's the correct way. But ask a hundred civilians to make the 'handcuff me' gesture, and they do it the way they see it on TV."

"Which way is that?"

"They make their hands into fists, thumbs to the side, and way too far apart."

He smiles. "What else do TV cops do wrong?"

"Don't get me started!"

"Seriously."

I shrug. "On TV they always lean the suspects over a car or against a building, or fence."

"So?"

"The suspect's best chance to make his move is while the officer's preparing to put the cuffs in place."

"Why's that?"

"There's an art to cuffing a suspect. On TV, they slap the cuffs on in a fraction of a second. In real life, it's a process. It's hard to secure a suspect with one hand, while retrieving and putting cuffs on with the other. If you lean the suspect against a solid surface, he can use it to push off, and throw you off-balance."

"What's the proper way?" he asks, obviously amused.

"In real life you want to keep the suspect off-balance. I want him on the ground, on his stomach, hands behind his back so I can press my knee into his back to maintain control. But if I have to cuff him upright, I make him spread his legs far apart—"

"Wait! I'll handcuff *you!*"

"—Let's ask Melanie what she thinks."

"I was just kidding. Tell me the rest."

"When the suspect's legs are spread wide apart, I have him raise one hand and put the other one behind his back. That makes it harder for him to get leverage."

"And if he tries to make a move just before you cuff him?"

"I can kick him in the nuts."

"Ouch!" he says.

"Exactly."

"I'll keep all this in mind," he says, "if I ever break the law."

"If you ever get caught, you mean."

"Anything else you want to tell me about handcuffs?" he asks, slyly.

"They can cause tissue and nerve damage if they're not applied properly. Older ones are easier to escape from than new ones. And you typically only cuff three types of people from the front. One? Pregnant women. Two? Suspects with medical conditions..."

"And the third?"

I look him in the eyes. "Juveniles."

"Ah," he says.

"Ah, indeed."

He pauses a moment, then says, "I probably knew about the handcuffing because my dad's an attorney. A very high-powered one."

"So I've heard."

He smirks. "What else have you heard?"

"I heard you were in Kelli Underhill's home Saturday night."

He's caught off guard, but recovers nicely. "Who told you that?"

"It's all over school."

"What do you mean?"

"The party."

"What party?"

"You, Ronnie, eight other boys. Kelli let you in just before midnight. You went down to the basement to hang out. Sometime after midnight you, and possibly Ronnie, snuck away from the others and went upstairs, to Kelli's bedroom."

He stares at me. Wants to hear me out, but wants to deny it, too. "Whoever told you that is full of shit."

"You weren't at Kelli's Saturday night?"

He says nothing for twenty seconds, during which I can practically see the wheels turning in his head while he thinks it over. According to Riley, there were ten boys there, and five girls. Too many people. He knows he can't deny it.

"Yeah, I went to Kelli's. Like you said, a bunch of us did. But I don't know anything about Kelli's bedroom. Why would I go upstairs? The party was in the basement."

"Maybe you wanted to molest the underage girl who passed out on the bed."

The look on his face speaks volumes. So does his sudden flash of temper.

"Get out!" he yells. "I'm calling my dad."

As he grabs his cell phone, I hand him my card, open the passenger door, and say, "Give your dad a message for me, okay?"

He glares at me. "Gladly, bitch."

"Tell him I said *strawberry*."

I slam the door shut.

He jumps out the driver's side. "Wait!"

I turn around, note the genuine fear in his face.

"What do you want, Dani?"

"Justice."

"How much do you know?"

"Enough to talk to the cops."

We stare at each other a moment. Then, to my complete surprise, his face breaks out in a wide grin.

"Why so happy, Ethan? Looking forward to jail time?"

"I'm a juvenile, Dani. And good luck proving anyone was molested, or that I was anywhere near Kelli's bedroom that night. If you had anything substantial, I'd be talking to the police right now, instead of you. Which tells me you've got nothing. What do I have? A house full of witnesses who will testify I was in the basement the entire time."

I want to give him a smart-ass reply, but my phone rings. I click off the recorder app, check the caller ID.

It's Rick Hooper.

"See you in court, Ethan."

"Until then, Sugar Tits," he says, grinning.

I get in my car, accept the call. "What's up, Rick?"

"Are you at your computer?"

"No. Why?"

"A friend just forwarded me a photo of Riley Freeman."

"Can you describe it?"

"She's lying on a bed, sleeping."

"Could she be passed out?"

"You know she is."

"Is she dressed?"

"Yes."

"Who's your friend?"

"Just a guy. He's not involved."

"Can you send it to me? My email's on my business card."

"My friend says there are a dozen more pictures floating around."

"Can you get him to send them to me?"

"He doesn't have them. Like I said, he's not involved. He just got the one, and sent it to me. But he heard there are more, and I believe him."

"Did he hear what type of pictures they were?"

"The bad kind."

I sigh. "It's time to tell me about the conversation you heard at school on Monday."

"Why?"

"Because the cops will be all over this by tomorrow."

He pauses a minute. Then says, "Okay. When?"

"Right now."

Chapter 13

"I only heard a small part of the conversation," Rick says.

"Just tell me what you know for certain."

"I heard a guy talking on his cell phone behind me at lunch."

"What guy?"

"Nathan Cain. I'm not sure who he was talking to."

"But you heard Nathan's part of the conversation clearly?"

"I've got this move where I put ear buds in my ears so people think I'm listening to music. But in reality there are holes in the ear buds, and I can hear everything people are saying around me!"

That is so pathetic I don't know how to respond. Then it dawns on me he wants me to agree it's a cool move. Before I can form the words, he says, "Nathan was telling the guy about how he and a bunch of guys went to Kelli Underhill's house Saturday night."

"Go on."

"He said while everyone else was drinking in the basement, Ethan and Ronnie scouted the house and found Riley Freeman passed out in the upstairs bedroom."

"What else did he say?"

"He said they climbed in the bed with her, to take a picture, as a joke, and before they knew it, she was all over them."

He pauses.

I frown. "Did he say anything else?"

"He said she was totally out of it. Said she kept telling them she loved them, and wanted to have a threesome. He said she took off her clothes, then passed out again. Ethan and Ronnie didn't say anything about it at the party, but later, in the car, they told everyone she had a sticker on her...um..."

"Private area?"

"Yeah. A strawberry. So that was going to be her new nickname."

"That story's bullshit, Rick."

"Are you going to tell the police?"

"Not yet. I need more evidence of a crime."

I think a minute, then say, "Rick?"

"Yeah?"

"Are you home right now?"

"Uh huh."

"Can I come over?"

"*Hell* yeah!"

"Give me your address."

He does.

I call Dillon. When he answers, I say, "I need you to meet me at Rick Hooper's house."

"When?"

"Right now."

"Is this for the case you took that pays us nothing?"

"Yeah. But it's going to be high-profile."

I give him Rick's address, and tell him to meet me there in fifteen minutes.

"What should I bring?"

"A bunch of equipment."

"What kind?"

"How should I know? You're the expert."

I hear him munching something that requires an inordinate amount of chewing before he finally swallows. When at last he speaks, his voice drips with condescension.

"Dani," he says, "I'm going to attempt to explain this in a way that makes sense to you."

"Thank you, Dillon."

"Would you use your hairbrush to clip your toenails?"

I take a deep breath. "No, Dillon, I would not."

"If you and Sophie are going out tonight, and you need a little extra padding in your bra, would you expect her to hand you a curling iron?"

I sigh. "No, Dillon, I wouldn't. And while we're at it, I wouldn't put my lipstick on with a rolling pin, though if I *had* a rolling pin I might be inclined to shove it up your skinny, pimpled ass right now. What's your point?"

"The equipment I bring depends on the job you need me to do."

"Why didn't you say that in the first place?"

"What do you need me to do?"

I tell him about the email Rick received from his friend.

"What about it?" he says.

"I want you to get on Rick's computer and track where it came from."

"Just have him forward it to me. I can backtrack the origin from my own computer."

"Aha!"

"Aha? What the hell is *that* supposed to mean?"

"It means I'm about to give you a revelation."

"This should be interesting."

"The problem with tracking it from *your* computer, you won't be able to check *Rick's* computer to see if he's already stored some additional photos of Riley on it."

"You think he has?"

"No, but it can't hurt to check."

"Fine. In that case I'll bring nothing with me."

"Why not?"

"All I need is Rick's computer."

"Fine. I'll see you there."

"Fine."

For some reason I find myself wanting to say "Fine!" again. But I resist the urge. I'm a professional, after all.

As I end the call, another one comes in. I don't recognize the number.

"Hello?"

"Ms. Ripper, this is Allen Roemer, Lydia Underhill's attorney."

"How can I help you?"

"By answering a simple question."

"Shoot."

"Is this whole thing some sort of joke?"

"What whole thing?"

"Your so-called investigation."

"It's not a formal investigation, but I'd love to speak to the Underhills. Can you arrange that?"

"No. But I can arrange a critical meeting with you at my office tomorrow morning."

"Why?"

"My clients are considering pressing charges."

"Against Ethan Clark?"

"No. You."

"Will Lydia be there?"

"Assuredly."

"Great! What time?"

"Nine o'clock."

"Can we meet at the Underhill's?"

"No chance in hell."

"Will Mr. Underhill be there?"

"I've invited all the Underhills."

"Kelli too?"

"Yes. But I'm not sure she can make it. It's a school day, after all."

That's him, reminding me she's a minor. I didn't get a chance to give Ethan a smart-ass reply earlier, so I'd like to make one now, to the Underhill's attorney.

But why bother?

After all, by setting up a meeting at his office with his clients, Mr. Roemer's playing right into my hands.

Chapter 14

When Rick opens the door and sees Dillon standing beside me, his face drops.

It drops even further when he hears I want Dillon to access his computer.

"My parents aren't here," he says.

"In that case, there's no one to interrupt us," I say.

Dillon sits at Rick's desk, makes a derogatory remark about the archaic keyboard, then starts clicking keys. Watching Dillon at work is like watching a master. Within seconds, his fingers are a blur. Ramsey Lewis couldn't do better work with a keyboard.

It takes him two minutes to find out the "friend" who forwarded Riley's photo is Nathan Cain, the guy Rick supposedly overheard in the lunch room.

"I can explain," Rick says.

"Let's talk in the hall," I say, knowing Dillon can work more effectively if Rick isn't looking over his shoulder.

He glances nervously at Dillon, who takes the cue and gets up from Rick's computer, crosses the room, sits on the side of Rick's bed, as if planning to wait there till we return.

I secretly press a button on the cell phone in my jeans pocket while escorting Rick out of the room. Then raise it an inch out of my pocket so the speaker can pick up our conversation. This way Dillon can hear everything Rick and I say, and Rick won't hear Dillon typing on his keyboard.

"Tell me about Nathan," I say, leading Rick down the hall.

"He's not really my friend," Rick says. "I exaggerated that part."

"You said he wasn't involved."

"That's what he told me."

"Then how could he send you the picture?"

"Nathan said Ethan and Ronnie took nude pictures of Riley with their cell phones. That night in the car, the guys believed them. But by Monday everyone doubted their story. So Ethan and Ronnie texted some of the photos to their closest friends and told them to keep it quiet. But who could keep that type of secret? It became a status symbol to have the pictures, so I begged Nathan to send me one."

"And he did."

"Yeah, but it cost me fifty bucks. And, he sent me the one where she was dressed."

"I don't believe this!" I say.

"What?"

"You paid him for a photo *after* I talked to you."

He looks down at the floor. Then says, "Like I said, it turned into a status symbol."

"And you'd do anything to fit in."

"Don't judge me. You don't know what it's like."

"If *you've* got a photo, the pictures must be all over the school by now."

"That's a cruel thing to say."

"Whine all you like. I'm disappointed in you, Rick."

"Of *course* you are. Why *wouldn't* you be? I'm a loser. Ask anyone."

"Don't lay that on me. It's a copout."

"What do you mean?"

"If you're a loser it's because you're acting like one. Get a grip. You want to change your status? Change your behavior."

A sound comes from my cell phone. It's Dillon, shouting, "Eureka!"

Rick and I go back to his room.

"You found the pictures?" I say.

"No, but they're being sent even as we speak," Dillon says.

"Explain."

"When I heard Rick say he paid Nathan fifty bucks for a photo, I live-chatted with Nathan. He's sending me the rest of the pictures."

Rick says, "Why would he send them to *you?*"

"I used your email account. He thought he was talking to you."

"Why would he send *me* the photos?"

"You offered to pay him a thousand dollars for them."

"*What?* I don't have that kind of money!"

"Then I guess you're screwed."

Rick looks at his computer screen, terrified and excited at the same time.

"Don't look here for them," Dillon says. "They're being sent to a disposable phone."

"I don't even know what that means," Rick says.

Dillon places a cheap cell phone next to the one he was using to take my call. "These are pre-paid cell phones," Dillon says. "They're anonymous."

He points to the second one. "I gave Nathan *this* number and told him it was yours. Except I don't know what's taking so long."

Rick says, "Dani, I don't *have* a thousand bucks! What am I gonna do when Nathan asks for the money? He's gonna *kill* me!"

I say, "Buy some time. Tell him you can't go to the bank till Friday to get the cash. By Friday, getting paid will be the last thing on Nathan's mind."

"What do you mean?"

"When he sends those photos, he'll be trafficking underage porn."

We stand around, twiddling our thumbs for five minutes.

"Something's wrong," Dillon says. "I can feel it."

He punches out a text message, presses the "send" button, and says, "I just asked him to hurry up."

Another five minutes pass, then the phone vibrates.

"Finally!" I say.

He picks the phone up, checks the screen, says, "Shit."

"What's wrong?"

"Someone got to him."

"What do you mean?"

"Nathan just sent a message. Said there *are* no other pictures of Riley."

"Read me his exact words."

Dillon reads, "There are no other pictures, asshole. I was joking."

I shake my head.

"You're right," I say. "Ethan called him. I shouldn't have confronted him. I tipped my hand."

"Not your fault," Dillon says. "You didn't know about the pictures when you talked to him."

I give Rick a withering look. "If you would have told me about the pictures yesterday, I could have used that to our advantage."

"We still can," Dillon says. "It's just that we won't have the element of surprise."

"How?"

"If they were ever taken on a cell phone, we can find them. Eventually."

Chapter 15

It's dark when I park in Sophie's driveway.

I've got a key to the front door, but I'm so busy digging it out of my handbag it doesn't dawn on me that most of the lights in the house are off.

Until I'm inside, with the door closed behind me.

By then it's too late.

The muffled noise and simultaneous pain in my side help me realize I've just been shot. I cry out, but before I can react, I'm hit two more times.

Shoulder and stomach.

My knees buckle. I fall to the floor in slow motion, and land in a sitting position. Gravity slowly takes over, forces me onto my back.

In the darkness I hear Sophie say, "You're still breathing, bitch. I can hear you. But that won't last for long."

She gloats, "I can't believe how *easy* this was! I don't mean pulling the trigger. I mean, you just walked right in, stood there like a deer in the headlights. I could have put one between your eyes, ended it once and for all. But this is better. So much better."

I turn my head in the direction of her voice, but don't see her.

She says, "I'm going to stand over you and watch you bleed out. When the light comes on, if you're able to turn your head upward, you'll see I'm completely naked. Want to know why, bitch? It keeps the blood evidence off my clothes. While you're lying there helplessly, struggling to gasp your final breaths, I'll be smearing your blood all over my body. I'm going to bathe myself with your hot, bitch blood."

I concentrate all my power into forming a sentence. "You're...completely insane. You'll never...get away...with it."

"I could kill you now, bitch. You know it's true. I have all the power. Say it! Tell me I have all the power."

I say nothing.

"*Say it!*" she screams, "or I swear I'll shoot you right now!"

The light comes on and I see Sophie standing over me, naked, holding a gun.

A nerf gun.

We both pause a moment, then laugh hysterically.

"*Hot, bitch blood?*" I say.

She laughs, shoots me in the arm.

"Was 'hot, bitch blood' too over the top?" she says.

"A bit. Maybe."

We laugh some more.

I say, "What possessed you to get naked and attack me with a toy gun?"

"You've been preoccupied like crazy. I wanted to get your attention."

"It worked."

"So," she says. "You want to fool around?"

"I'm not gay, Sophie."

"Who said you were?"

She places her hand between my legs, rubs my sweet spot.

I feel my body surrender. She straddles me, unbuttons my shirt. Cups my breast. Lowers her face till our lips are inches apart. I lift my chin to accept her kiss.

We pause to take a breath and I say, "I just wanted to be clear."

"About not being gay?"

"Yes."

I put my arms around her, caress her lower back with my fingertips.

We kiss again.

She says, "Noted."

Chapter 16

Thursday.

Dillon's call wakes me up at two a.m.

"Are you serious, Dillon? What could you possibly want at this hour?"

"We've got a problem."

I wipe the sleep from my eyes. "What?"

"I got a beep on my tracking program."

"At two in the morning?"

"It's Jana Bagger."

"What about her?"

"Her car just stopped at Fourteen Twenty-Six Riverside."

"Why does that address sound familiar?"

"It's her husband's other house. The one he shares with Darcie Darden."

"Shit!"

"Should I call the cops?"

"No."

"Because?"

"Because what if she kills someone and they find the tracking device you put in her car?"

"That would be bad, I suppose."

"Really? Ya think?"

"What should we do?"

I waste several precious seconds, trying to think it through. Then say, "You've still got Max's car bugged, right?"

"Uh huh."

"Is he there?"

"Yup."

"Shit."

"You said that."

"I'll say it again, I expect."

"Maybe she's doing her own surveillance," Dillon says.

"Or maybe she's waiting for him to come out so she can shoot him."

"We need to get the tracking devices from their cars," Dillon says.

"I agree. What are you, fifteen minutes from Darcie's?"

"Yeah, probably."

"I can be there in twenty."

"Want me to meet you out front?"

"No. We should arrive together. Park your car two blocks before you get to Darcie's. I'll look for you."

"There's a convenience store just off the interstate, right-hand side."

"Okay, I'll meet you there."

"Dani?"

"Yeah?"

"Bring your gun this time, okay?"

"I can't."

He sighs. "Why not?"

"It's in my desk drawer. At the office."

"Shit."

"That's my line."

Chapter 17

It's over by the time we get there.

Neighbors are on the perimeter, speaking in hushed tones. Max and Jana are in the front yard, but only one of them is alive.

Max.

"Are you with the police?" he says, as I approach, carrying a flashlight.

"No. Have you called them?"

"Yes."

I glance down the street where Dillon's already managed to open Jana's trunk. We're lucky she parked a good distance away. But I have no idea what to do about the bug Dillon planted in Max's car.

Speaking of Max, he's crying.

"What happened here?" I say.

He points at the shattered glass near the front door and says, "My wife tried to shoot us through the window."

I look at Jana's body. "If that's true, she must be the worst shot in history."

"She fired twice. The second shot must have ricocheted on something."

"Wait. You're claiming she shot *herself*?"

"She *must* have. Darcie and I don't own guns. But neither does Jana."

"Where's the gun she used?"

"Next to her body, I suppose. This is as close as I've gotten to her."

"Because?"

"I was afraid she might be faking, hoping I'd come closer so she could shoot me."

I shine my flashlight on her body. If there's a gun, it's under her.

"You're sure Jana doesn't own a gun?"

"We don't believe in them. But she sure as hell had one. This is crazy. It's crazy."

He looks at me. Says, "Who are you, exactly?"

"Dani Ripper. Your wife hired me to find out if you were cheating on her."

Something bubbles up inside him. His face twists with rage.

"This is *your* fault!" he shouts, and punches my face so fast and hard I fly six feet through the air before my back slams against the ground. He starts coming at me, but thankfully two of the neighbors come running to my rescue.

"Are you all right?" first guy says.

I murmur something.

Second guy asks, "What did she say?"

"She said she hates her job."

"What's her job?"

First guy leans closer and says, "What's your job, hon?"

"From now on? I'm a decoy."

"You mean like duck hunters use?"

"Yeah. That's exactly what I mean," I say, rubbing my jaw.

"What'd she say?" second man yells.

"She says she's a duck hunter!"

Chapter 18

"Dani, hi. Everything okay?"

I'm on the phone with my favorite assassin, Donovan Creed. Yes, I said "favorite." I actually know more than one assassin.

Impressed?

I say, "Donovan, I've got a situation."

"I love situations," he says. "How can I help?"

"I need some advice."

"Oh."

He sounds disappointed. "Hypothetically, if a friend of yours put a tracking device in a car, and that car is currently part of a crime scene, and your friend didn't want the cops to find it, what would you do?"

"Hypothetically, where is the car, exactly? On the street, in a driveway, in a garage?"

"Let's say it's in a garage that's attached to a house."

"In a neighborhood? In Nashville?"

"A ritzy neighborhood in Nashville, where the houses are several hundred feet apart. Hypothetically."

"Give me a hypothetical address, and within two hours I'll have my guy blow the garage to hell."

"Are you serious?"

"Do you really have to ask me that?"

God, I love this guy. It occurs to me to clarify, "No one gets hurt, right?"

He pauses. "Is that how you want it?"

"Yes."

"I'll do it anyway."

Chapter 19

Despite the fact she's a minor, and should be in school, Kelli Underhill's sitting at the client conference table.

Also present are her mother, Lydia, and their attorney, Allen Roemer.

Roemer motions me to take a seat. I start to, and he says, "Not there."

I pull out a different chair, and he says, "Not there, either."

Two chairs remain. I pick one.

"Not that one," he says.

There are one million two hundred thousand attorneys in this country, which means six hundred thousand of them graduated in the bottom-half of their class. Why do I always wind up with that bunch?

After I sit, Roemer clears his throat and says, "Before I start threatening you, is there anything you'd like to say?"

"Yes."

"Go ahead, then."

"On the first day of school, a first-grade teacher tells her class they're not babies anymore. They have to use grown up words. Then she asks the kids what they did that summer. The first kid says, 'I got a bad boo boo.' Teacher says, 'No. You suffered an injury. Use grown up words.' Second kid says, 'I rode on a choo choo.' Teacher says, 'No. You rode on a train. Use grown up words.' Third kid says, 'I read a book.' Teacher says, 'Good for you! Which book did you read?' The kid says, 'Uh...Winnie the Shit!'"

All three of them stare at me slack-jawed.

Roemer says, "What the hell are you *talking* about?"

"I was telling you a joke."

"A joke," he repeats.

"That's right."

"Why?"

"Because when I told Lydia her daughter and her friends were drinking Saturday night, she said, 'Obviously, this is a joke.' When I told her Kelli let boys in the house, she said, 'Seriously, Ms. Ripper. Is this your idea of a joke?' And when you called me yesterday afternoon the first thing you said was, 'Ms. Ripper, is this whole thing some sort of joke?' I just wanted you to hear what a joke actually sounds like, so you'd know the difference."

"Don't give up your day job," he says.

"Too late."

Kelli says, "What happened to your face?"

"Let's just say I lost another client."

Roemer says, "I saw it on the news. Your client shot herself while trying to kill her husband."

"That's what they're saying."

"Then he assaulted you in front of numerous witnesses. This morning, he publicly accused you of blowing up his garage. Except that you were being treated at the hospital when the explosion occurred."

"Is there a question coming my way?"

"Are you planning to file a lawsuit?"

"Why, do you want to represent me?"

"That would be unethical, unless today's business is quickly resolved."

"Speaking of which..." I say.

"I want you to stop all this nonsense," he says. "What were you *thinking?*"

"The same stuff I'm *still* thinking. Lydia? Where's your husband?"

Roemer says, "Out of town."

"He's out of town a lot," I say.

"Thank God for that," Kelli says, under her breath.

Lydia places her hand firmly on her daughter's forearm.

I say, "I'm guessing he's your stepdad?"

She nods.

Lydia says, "How did you arrive at that conclusion?"

"I'm a student of people," I say. "A master of logic. A professor of deductive reasoning."

"You asked around," Roemer says.

"That, too."

Roemer clears his throat again and says, "Kelli has admitted a small amount of controlled drinking took place at her home Saturday night, and that she did, in fact, allow a small number of classmates into her home to talk about

93

schoolwork. They were quiet and respectful, and left a few minutes later in an orderly fashion."

I look at Kelli and say, "See? This is why we need lawyers."

Roemer says, "Is it true you're claiming a young lady was molested at the Underhill residence Saturday night?"

"I'm investigating a *possible* molestation."

"Riley Freeman?"

I decide not to respond.

Roemer says, "Do you have the slightest shred of evidence a crime occurred?"

"That depends on what you call evidence."

"The courts are quite clear as to what constitutes evidence."

"I bet thousands of inmates would dispute that claim."

"Nevertheless, evidence must be credible. And legally obtained."

I say, "The most common form of evidence is witness testimony, correct?"

"It is," he says. "Do you have any?"

"Sort of."

"Then why haven't you gone to the police?"

"I'm building a case."

"You've been retained by Claire Freeman, Riley's mother?"

I decide not to answer.

"Reason I'm asking, she doesn't seem to know anything about it."

I feel the blood draining from my face. "You told her what happened to *Riley?*"

"Relax. I simply asked if she had retained you, and she said no. I told her I'd been misinformed, and that was that. Which begs the question, for whom are you working?"

"Truth, justice, and the American way," I say.

We stare at each other until he says, "How much do you know about libel and slander?"

"In layman's terms?"

"If you must."

"I must."

"Go ahead."

"Libel is defamation in print or pictures. Slander is oral defamation."

"Spoken like a true layman"

"But generally true?"

"Here's a better question," he says. "Are you prepared to defend yourself in court for defaming the Underhills?"

"I haven't defamed anyone, yet. Certainly not the Underhills."

"Guess again."

"I've got a girl who says something may have happened to her. I'm trying to find out if it's true."

"So your client is Riley Freeman? A minor?"

"Is there a law against it?"

"Probably. I'll have to check. More importantly, you just admitted your client doesn't even know if something happened to her."

To Kelli I say, "Your bedroom's on the second floor, right? And the master bedroom's on the main floor?"

She nods and is about to say something, but her mother squeezes her arm.

"I'll take that as a yes," I say.

Roemer sees me fiddling with my cell phone and says, "What have you got there?"

I hand him my phone and say, "How would you interpret this photo?"

He takes a moment to study the picture of Riley that Rick Hooper sent me. Then he says, "A young lady in her pajamas napping peacefully on a bed at an undisclosed location."

"That's what I'd say, too, if I were you. Except that this photo was taken at the Underhill home shortly after midnight last Saturday. It was taken by a boy who entered the Underhill home. A boy who created a nickname for Riley, and spread it throughout the school."

"What nickname is that?"

"Strawberry."

"I suppose you're dying to tell me why?"

"Before going to the sleepover, Riley Freeman, for her own personal reasons, affixed a tiny strawberry sticker east of her labia."

"East?"

"I'm trying to be delicate."

"Are you also trying to make a point?"

"I am. Riley told no one about the sticker. Not even her best friend. And yet, the boy who took this photo, and other, more revealing photos, gave her that nickname."

"So?"

"If he never saw her naked, what made him give her that nickname?"

He shakes his head. "That's all you've got? Maybe she likes strawberries. Maybe she hates them. Maybe she has a red birthmark on her elbow."

"Her elbow?"

"It could mean anything."

"What about the photos?"

"Do you have any proof they exist?"

"Just hearsay, at this point."

He shakes his head again. "Dani, you've been hoodwinked."

"Hoodwinked?"

"Duped," he says. "Deceived. In layman's terms, you've been tricked."

"How so?"

"An attorney would argue she did, in fact, tell someone. If, as you say, she was inebriated at the time, who's to say she didn't have a short conversation with the person who snapped the picture? And why wouldn't she tell that person about the strawberry sticker? Meanwhile, you're publicly discussing the possible molestation of a minor at the Underhill's home. You're casting my clients in a criminally negligent light."

"How much better will the light be when a group of photos surface, proving an underage girl was molested at your client's home?"

"It's not going to get that far because we don't believe these photos exist. But your irresponsible public comments that a crime took place in my clients' home, under Mrs. Underhill's personal supervision, has already caused irreparable damage to her reputation and standing in the community."

"Fancy language aside, what's your actual threat?"

"Mrs. Underhill, against my strong recommendation to the contrary, is willing to sweep your slanderous, libelous actions aside, provided you immediately cease your investigation."

"Is that it?"

"No. I'll require you to sign a statement to the effect you were mistaken in your conclusions, that your investigation focused entirely on the hearsay of children outside the presence of adults, that it was ill-advised, careless, flawed, and that you apologize for your irresponsible and outrageous public remarks."

"I assume you've already drafted the letter?"

"As a matter of fact, I have."

He removes a letter from his valise and says, "This is your lucky day, Ms. Ripper. My client has given you a free pass. A gift."

"Against your better judgment."

"That's right. I have a strong feeling she'll regret this. Sign at the bottom, please, when you're ready."

We stare at each other a minute. Then I say, "Got a pen?"

"I do."

He hands me a pen, I use it.

He collects the paper and says, "You got off lucky this time, Ms. Ripper. You should go out and buy a lottery ticket."

I stand.

He looks at my signature and frowns.

As I head for the door I notice Kelli and Lydia checking to see what I wrote on the signature line: *Is this some sort of joke?*

Chapter 20

My entire case hangs on a rumor.

Are nude pictures of Riley floating around in cyberspace? I hope so.

Wait. That sounds really bad. You know what I mean, right?

What I'm saying, if there are no nude photos, Riley has no case. As Roemer just proved, everything that's happened can easily be explained away by a competent defense attorney.

Not to mention I could lose my license and have my ass handed to me by a number of attorneys, including Ethan Clark's father.

What we have here is the absence of photos, which in lawyer-speak means, there was no crime. I mean, I know there was a crime, and I can narrow the suspects to fifteen, if we can agree there were ten boys, a mom, and four girls besides Riley.

Speaking of the mom, Lydia Underhill, could there be a reason her husband, Mitch, is out of town? Could they be separated?

Is Mitch, a possible suspect? Is that why he's not around?

This is what's crazy about my job: you have to suspect everyone.

Having said that, my gut feeling on Lydia is she's a good parent who probably didn't want Kelli to have a sleepover that night. She probably relented because arguing with Kelli about it wasn't worth the hassle. As a former teen, this is an easy conclusion to draw. I had a mom, I know the drill.

I also believe Lydia when she says Kelli isn't the type to steal liquor from her parents, or allow friends to drink in her home, or open the door to boys at such a late hour.

So what factor created these circumstances?

I have no idea. But one possibility is Kelli's stepdad has moved out.

Maybe he's run off with his secretary, or perhaps he and Lydia are undergoing a trial separation. Maybe Saturday night Lydia was upset about the situation with her husband, and didn't feel like having girls in the house. Maybe that's why she retreated to the bedroom and closed the door.

Lydia strikes me as a responsible parent. I doubt under normal circumstances she'd close herself up in an upstairs bedroom while teenage girls were awake in the house.

Did Lydia go to the room to cry about the current state of her marriage? Did she turn on the TV so no one would hear her crying? Did she close the door so no one would see her drinking?

All these things are possible. Otherwise, how could she not know Parker's mother arrived at midnight to collect her daughter? How could she not hear ten boys in her house? How could she be completely oblivious that kids were going up and down the back stairs, or that Riley spent the entire night in Kelli's room, and may have been molested?

And why would Lydia sleep in an upstairs bedroom anyway? The master bedroom's on the main floor. Could she have moved upstairs because her husband's gone and she wants to be closer to Kelli?

You probably think I'm making too much out of the fact Mitch has been gone for at least five days. After all, lots of husbands travel, and Mitch has been gone less than a week, as far as I know. But if you could have seen the way Lydia and Kelli looked at each other when I asked about him, and the way Kelli muttered, "Thank God for that" when I mentioned him being out of town, and the way Lydia looked at me yesterday when she asked how I knew her husband—you'd understand why it gives me pause.

Not that any of this matters, because Ethan Clark's our guy.

I'm sure of it.

I've had a lot of "hands on" experience with predators. I've spent years evaluating them, following their trails of terror. Ethan Clark's good-looking, wealthy, has a smooth rap, and his creep factor is off the charts. The way he boldly stared at my chest? I'm not exactly well-endowed, nor was I dressed sexily. I was wearing a nondescript business suit.

Which is why I didn't describe it to you earlier.

And let's not forget Ethan's comment about how many hours he spent searching the internet for nude pictures of me.

Nude pictures?

Does that ring a bell?

And another thing: every predator I've ever met or studied had a Jekyll and Hyde personality. During our brief meeting yesterday, Ethan Clark displayed a host of emotions. He was brash, condescending, angry, frightened, arrogant.

Of course all these things and a nickel buys me a nickel's worth of manure.

I need the photos.

They're as critical as Monika Lewinski's dress. Without the dress, there was no affair.

Am I saying I need a blue dress slathered in semen?

In a way, yes.

Which is why the whole time I was meeting with Mr. Roemer and the Underhills, Dillon was breaking into Kelli's home, searching her bedroom, photographing every inch of it.

What do we expect to find?

Nothing.

Something.

Everything.

We need any type of evidence that will give credence to, or dispute, Riley's story.

As I wait for Dillon to answer his phone, Roemer's words play through my mind.

Evidence must be credible, and legally obtained.

Whatever Dillon finds might be credible, but...

"You're done?" Dillon says. "The meeting's over already?"

"It is. What have you found?"

"Nothing. But I took lots of pictures."

"Can you tell if Mitch Underhill is still living there?"

"To tell you the truth, pasting isn't the only thing I suck at. I'm even worse at breaking and entering. I've only been inside for ten minutes."

"Well, we tried."

"I need to get out of here. My car's a half-mile away."

"Come straight to the office, okay? I'd like to see what Kelli's room looks like."

Chapter 21

We're at my office, looking at pictures of Kelli's bedroom on my computer screen. Riley's with us.

"You took these with a *cell* phone?" Riley says.

Dillon laughs. "No way! Nikon D7000."

As I flip from one picture to the next, I ask, "Who brought you here today?"

"My mom."

"She knows you're meeting me?"

"No, ma'am. She drops me off at the mall. I tell her I'm hanging out with friends. I go in the front, walk out the back. It's only ten minutes."

I ask if she was wearing socks Saturday night (Yes). Slippers? (No). Did she pass out with her socks on? (Yes). I ask if she turned down the bedspread. (No). I ask if there's any way she might have disrobed during the night, and was it possible she woke up for a few minutes when Ethan and Ronnie were in the room with her. (No and no).

I ask if there's anything she can remember about that night she hasn't told us, or anything she can think of to help us prove her story.

As expected, she's got nothing new to add, so I say, "Tell me about Kelli's relationship with her stepfather, Mitch."

"She hates him."

"Why?"

She bites her lip. "I'm not sure."

The way she says it tells me she absolutely *does* know.

"It could be important," I say.

She says nothing.

"Has Mitch moved out of the house?"

"No, ma'am."

"How long has he been out of town?"

"He left Saturday morning."

"Any idea when he's coming back?"

"Saturday, I think."

"Does he travel often?"

"I'm not sure. We don't really talk about him."

"Because?"

"They don't get along."

"Does Mitch get along with Lydia?"

"They sleep in separate bedrooms."

"How long has that been going on?"

"I don't know. A long time, I think."

Dillon says, "She doesn't keep clothes in the guest bedroom. Just an alarm clock and a cell phone charger."

We come to the end of the photos.

Riley says, "Are the sleeping arrangements important?"

"Probably not," I say. "I'm just trying to understand their relationship."

She says, "Lydia sleeps upstairs when he's out of town. So she can be near Kelli. When Mitch is home, she sleeps in the master bedroom."

"And Mitch sleeps in the guest bedroom?"

"No. He has his own master bedroom upstairs."

I look at Dillon.

He says, "There were three bedrooms upstairs. I looked in all of them."

Riley says, "There's a fourth one. He keeps it locked."

Dillon thinks a minute. Then says, "Right. One of the doors was locked. I assumed it was storage."

"Seriously, Dillon?" I say.

"I was in a rush, Dani. It took me forever to get in the house. You said Kelli's room was the priority. I barely had time to photograph it, much less break into another room."

Riley says, "You broke into their *house?*"

I say, "How did you *think* we got the pictures?"

"I assumed Mrs. Underhill let you in."

"She did, in a manner of speaking."

"I don't understand."

Dillon says, "This ought to be interesting."

I say, "If she had done a better job of securing her home, Dillon couldn't have entered. And by not setting the alarm, and refusing to install stronger locks, she may as well have sent him an engraved invitation."

Riley frowns.

I add, "Is it *really* breaking and entering if he didn't go there to *steal* anything."

"Yes," Riley says.

I change the subject and ask, "Why does Mitch keep his bedroom locked?"

"I don't know, but he doesn't allow anyone in there. Ever."

Dillon and I exchange a look.

He shrugs. "Sorry, Dani. I didn't know."

I sigh.

"My case isn't looking very good, is it?" Riley says.

"Honestly? No. We really need the other photos."

Riley says, "I'm sorry, but I really hope there aren't any others."

"I understand," I say. "But if they did something to you and photographed it, we'd own them."

We're quiet a minute, then Riley says, "Do you really think they took other pictures? Because if they did, wouldn't they be all over the internet?"

"You'd think so. But Ethan's the son of a lawyer. He and Ronnie probably showed the pictures to the kids in the car, but I expect the only one he shared was the one where you're passed out."

"And you said that one doesn't help us."

"Well, it's certainly not worthless. It proves Ethan was in the room with you."

"But it doesn't prove I was unconscious at the time."

"Maybe not. But it might give a judge a reason to pursue the case."

"But naked pictures would be huge?"

"They would. And Ethan and Ronnie certainly took pictures of you. Rick overheard Nathan tell someone there

107

were a dozen photos. And Nathan came within an inch of sending them to Dillon before denying it."

Riley says, "If Ethan and Ronnie didn't share them, how could Nathan have them in the first place?"

Dillon and I look at each other.

He says, "You think all ten guys have the photos and are sitting on them?"

I say, "What I'd give to have Ethan's phone in my hand for ten minutes."

Dillon and I look at each other again. Thinking the same thing.

I say, "Riley. Are you guys allowed to have cell phones at school?"

"At school, yes. In class, no."

"Where do you keep your phones during class? In your lockers?"

"Yes, ma'am."

Dillon says, "Even if she gives us the locker numbers I'd never be able to cut the locks. I'd need a giant set of bolt cutters. There's no way I can smuggle them into the hallway of a private school."

Riley says, "We don't use locks."

"Excuse me?"

"We're not allowed to have locks in upper school. It's part of the honor code we sign each year."

I say, "Wait. Are you telling me you could open Ethan's locker any time you feel like it? You could just walk up and steal his cell phone?"

"*I* couldn't."

"Why not?"

"If they caught me I'd lose my scholarship. I'd never be able to get into a decent college. Even if I got the evidence you need, it wouldn't be worth getting expelled."

"Dillon and I can do it," I say. "If you can give us the locker numbers."

"All ten?"

"Just Ethan and Ronnie's."

"I can tell you right now. Mine is sixty-one. Ethan's is four past mine, number sixty-five. Ronnie's is the next one, sixty-six."

Dillon says, "Can you draw me a map of the hallways so I can get in and out quickly?"

"Sure."

I give her a pen and paper. While she sketches the layout, I ask, "Are there cameras in the hall where the lockers are?"

"No, ma'am."

"Are the schoolroom doors closed during classes?"

"Yes, ma'am."

"This is almost too easy," Dillon says.

"If Dillon walks through the hall while classes are underway, is he likely to run into anyone?"

"Probably not. Unless it's the headmaster or one of the secretaries. But their offices are on the other side of the building."

"There must be a lot of theft taking place," Dillon says.

She shakes her head, no. "We take our honor code very seriously."

"Except at slumber parties," I say.

"Except then," Riley says.

I look at Dillon. "What do you think?"

"I like it. If you've got my back."

"We'll go in together. Sophie and I will be your lookouts. If someone comes down the hall, we'll intercept them and strike up a conversation."

"Where are we likely to find the cell phones?" Dillon asks.

"In their backpacks at the bottom of the lockers," Riley says.

Dillon frowns. "I'd have to dig through their backpacks? That could take time."

"Our backpacks have a cell phone pocket on the right side. It'll take you five seconds, max."

"What's the best time tomorrow?" I ask.

She thinks a minute. "Eight-thirty."

"Why?"

"School starts at eight. Anyone who's late for school will be there by eight-ten, or they won't come till nine."

"Why not?"

"You're not allowed to enter a classroom more than ten minutes late. It's disruptive."

"I like this more and more," I say.

Riley says, "Also, at eight-thirty all the teachers will be busy with classes. The teachers don't start taking breaks till ten."

"Eight-thirty it is!" I say.

I notice Riley staring at my computer screen.

"Is something wrong?"

"No ma'am. But...could you go all the way back to the first four pictures? You sort of skipped over those."

"That's because they didn't turn out," I say.

"Sure they did," Dillon says. "It's just that I took them before turning on the lights."

"Why?"

"To test the flash."

I scroll back to the beginning.

She takes a long, hard look at two of the photos.

"Do you see something?" I say.

She looks a few more seconds, then says, "I guess not. They just look different, is all. I'd best head back to the mall."

We stand. "Thanks for coming, Riley. Maybe we'll get lucky tomorrow morning with the cell phones."

She studies my face a minute. "I can't believe someone punched you like that."

"I know, right? For the first time in years, guys are actually staring at my face."

Chapter 22

Friday.

Dillon, Sophie, and I are in the hallway of Carson Collegiate, where, as promised, the upper school lockers are completely devoid of locks.

"The bell rings at eight-fifty-five," I remind Dillon. "When that happens, the halls will be crowded."

"Which means I've got twenty minutes," he says. "Don't worry, I set the alarm on my cell phone."

"You've got it on vibrate, I hope."

"Of course!" he says.

"Check it," I say.

He accesses his screen, frowns, and presses a button.

"Good to go," he says.

Sophie says, "That little exchange didn't inspire much confidence."

She and I split up and take our positions at opposite ends of the hall so we can warn Dillon if anyone approaches.

Riley was right.

Eight-thirty's a perfect time for the crime.

It takes Dillon less than three minutes to find both phones and walk fifteen steps to the boys' bathroom, where he plans to lock himself in one of the stalls while searching through Ethan and Ronnie's stored photographs.

I'm positive both boys took pictures of Riley. If so, they probably shared them, which means both phones are likely to contain the same photos. But Dillon will be able to tell which photos were taken from each phone, which will help us build a case against both boys when all this goes before a judge.

When Dillon finds the photos of Riley, he'll forward them to his phone, and we'll have our evidence. Then he'll wipe his fingerprints off the phones and put them back where he found them.

As the minutes pass, Sophie and I get increasingly nervous. We're both well-known in Nashville, and even though we're wearing wigs and ball caps, we feel as conspicuous as rats in a birdcage.

At the eighteen-minute mark I'm in full panic mode. I send Dillon a warning text. Seconds later, he exits the bathroom, puts the phones back in the lockers, and starts walking down the hall, toward Sophie, who's standing on the end closest to the exit. I start walking the same way, when the bell rings.

Within seconds the hallway fills, as kids spill out of classrooms like dice in a Yahtzee game.

I turn abruptly, and walk briskly, just short of a jog, toward the far side of the building. The faster I walk, the faster the blood pumps through my body, which makes the area around my eye ache from the blow I took yesterday.

I pass the upper school office and hear a lady say, "May I help you?"

I pretend I don't hear, and keep going.

As I approach the headmaster's office, the door opens, and two men come out. They shake hands, then turn to see me flying toward them. They both look me up and down, as if I've spilled gravy all over the front of my dress.

"Gentlemen," I say as I approach.

"Dani Ripper!" one of them says as I pass by.

I don't turn, don't slow down. Just head out the door and start walking around the building till I see Dillon's car coming toward me.

"Close call!" Sophie says.

I climb in the back seat. She opens the glove compartment and says, "You want your gun now?"

"Hell no! I hate that thing. It gives me the creeps."

"Would you rather have another black eye?"

Dillon says, "You can't keep it in *my* car. I don't have a permit."

"Fine," I say. "Give me the gun."

She does, and I slip it in my handbag. Then say, "Someone just made me."

"Even with the wig? Who?" Dillon says.

"I don't know. Distinguished guy coming out of the headmaster's office."

"So much for the disguise," Sophie says.

"Well, there wasn't much I could do with half my face swollen like this. Give me some good news, Dillon, my face hurts like hell."

They look at each other.

I say, "Good news, guys, nothing else."

No one speaks.

"Guys?" I say. "Quit kidding around. What did you get, Dillon?"

"Nothing," Dillon says.

"*What?*"

"Nothing *yet*," Sophie amends. "But there's still a chance."

"What do you mean?"

Dillon says, "I started with Ethan's phone. Searched for ten minutes, couldn't find any photos of Riley. I was running out of time, so I downloaded all the photos and videos on his phone to mine. Then did the same with Ronnie's phone."

"Okay, so you've got all their photos on your phone?"

"Yes. And their videos."

"Then it's just a matter of searching."

"Yeah, but I searched pretty well the first time. I started with the most recent and went back about four months. I didn't see any photos of Riley."

"Could they be stored in a hidden area?"

"I downloaded an app to their phones that pulls up every photo ever taken. Even photos they've taken in the past and erased."

"But you didn't have time to go through the entire file."

"No."

"And you haven't searched Ronnie's yet."

"No."

"Just to be clear, their entire photo files are on your phone."

"Yes. And videos."

"Find a place to pull over. We'll go through every picture, every video, one by one."

"Okay. But—"

"But what?"

"I've got a bad feeling about this."

Chapter 23

After reviewing the photos, I now know the man I saw at school talking to the headmaster was Gavin Clark, Ethan's father.

That's not particularly good news, but it beats the hell out of the bad news. The bad news is there were no photos of Riley on either phone.

Not one.

Nada.

Zip.

Zilch.

I can't tell you how devastated I am. Can't bear the thought of telling her.

We go through that whole process where Sophie and I ask the same questions a dozen different ways. "Are you absolutely certain you downloaded every photo from both phones?" (Yes). "Could there have been some sort of password-protected storage area within the phone you couldn't find?" (No).

"Could they have sent the photos to some other location, such as a porn site they could access whenever they wanted?" (Yes, but because of the app Dillon installed, the photos would still show up as having been taken by the cell phone cameras).

Sophie says, "Why was Ethan's father talking to the headmaster?"

"My guess? He's probably reminding him how much he and the other nine sets of parents donate to the school."

"In case it goes to court?"

"That's my guess."

"But if he knows there are no photos, why bother?"

"If Riley's mom goes to the police, they'll probably question everyone who was in Kelli's house that night. They might want to interview them at school. They may want character references from the headmaster and teachers, or at the very least, cooperation. Gavin Clark's a pro. He's probably hedging his bet."

My phone rings.

"It's Riley," I say. "Would either of you care to take the call?"

"No way!" Dillon says.

"Sophie?" I say.

"She doesn't even *know* me!"

"True."

I answer the phone saying, "Wish I had better news, honey."

Riley says, "You couldn't find the phones?"

"We did find them."

"Dillon checked the photo files?"

"He did. But found nothing."

She pauses a moment. "By nothing, you mean what, no nude photos?"

"No photos of any kind."

"There were no photos of me on *either* phone?"

"No. I'm so sorry, Riley. I feel terrible. I can't imagine how you must feel."

"Confused," she says. Then says something that stuns me. Something that reminds me that beyond the little girl innocence, the *yes, ma'am, no ma'am* Southern drawl politeness, there's a reason she's an honor student with a full academic scholarship.

She's brilliant.

So she makes the stunning comment, which is actually a question, and I say, "Shit! I can't believe we missed that! I'll pass it on to Dillon, and we'll talk to you after school."

"Want me to come to your office?"

"Can you?"

"I think so. Around four?"

"Perfect. See you then. And Riley?"

"Yes, ma'am?"

"If you ever want a summer job or need to do an internship, I get first dibs, okay?"

"Wow, thanks Ms. Ripper! That would be great!"

We hang up and Dillon says, "What was *that* all about?"

"Riley just asked me a hell of a question."

"Which is?"

"Pull over."

"Why?"

"I want to see the look on your face when I ask it."

"It won't be anything important," he says.

119

Sophie says, "Come on, Dillon, pull over! Dani's not always right, but she's always entertaining."

Dillon pulls over, puts the car in park, then turns to face me.

"Go ahead," he says, clearly annoyed.

As if he's the only genius in the world.

"Ask me her brilliant, amazing question."

"The app you installed can access every photo ever taken from Ethan's cell phone, right? Even if it's been erased?"

"I've told you that a hundred times."

"Yes, you have."

"So?"

"So—brace yourself—where's the picture of Riley passed out on the bed? The one we *know* he sent to Nathan Cain?"

My kickboxing coach says Teofilo Stevenson's punches had a concussive effect. Teo would catch you with a clean shot, but you'd keep fighting, as if nothing happened. Several seconds later, you'd stagger and crumple to the canvass. You'd been knocked out instantly, but it took a few seconds for your body to get the message. Riley's question caused that type of delayed reaction before showing up on Dillon's face, but those seconds have passed now, and his face is turning a dark shade of purple.

He closes his eyes, starts muttering.

Checks his phone.

When he's finally able to speak, he says, "Ethan's dad must know someone high up in government security."

"What do you mean?"

"Someone permanently erased all pictures of Riley. It's as if they were never taken in the first place."

"Why didn't you consider that possibility before now?"

"Because it's impossible."

Sophie says, "Obviously not. I bet they erased Riley's photos from all ten phones."

"All ten?" I say.

I think about it. "Well, why not? That's a lot of witnesses to keep up with. Gavin could have gotten all the guys together, rounded up all the cell phones, removed Riley's photos."

Sophie says, "They probably had a meeting, where all ten brought their cell phones. While someone erased them, Gavin rehearsed the boys on what to say to the cops."

"And me."

"And you."

Dillon says, "The technology you're talking about doesn't exist. How could they permanently remove selected photos and not all the others? This type of technology would have to be at the highest government security level."

Sophie says, "Would Ethan's dad have that type of pull?"

"I don't know," I say. "But according to Riley, he's a bigwig."

Dillon says, "I'd like to know if that sort of technology is even possible."

"It *has* to be," I say. "Otherwise, you'd have found the photo of Riley we already saw."

He looks at me. "Can you call your boyfriend?"

Sophie arches an eyebrow.

I wink at her, whip out my cell phone, call Donovan Creed.

Chapter 24

Creed says, "Dani, I pride myself on always being available for you, but I'm kind of busy right now, unless your life's in danger."

"Has something terrible happened?"

"I'll know more when we get there."

"Where?"

"Willow Lake, Arkansas. An entire neighborhood has just been blown off the map."

"Oh, my *God*, Donovan! Terrorists?"

"We don't know. Are you in danger?"

"No. I—look, please. I wish I hadn't called. I'm so sorry to bother you!"

"Just a sec," he says, covering the mouthpiece. I hear muffled conversation, then he says, "I'm on the tarmac, waiting to taxi. The pilot says I've got ninety seconds. What's up?"

"It seems so silly compared to—"

"Dani?"

"Yes?"

"Just tell me what you need."

I take a quick breath and say, "I've been told it's impossible to wipe selected photographs from a cell phone. In other words, to remove all traces of certain photos without affecting the others."

"That's bullshit. We've been doing it for years."

"Who's we?"

"Homeland Security. CIA. FBI. The Pentagon. It's not that big a deal."

"Could the average civilian do it?"

"No. These are classified programs."

"Quick question. If they've been wiped clean, is there any way to restore them?"

"Not if we erased them."

I pause a moment. He says, "Is that it?"

"Yes. I'm so sorry to bother you."

"No problem."

"Good luck, Donovan."

"You too."

I tell Dillon what Creed said.

"That is so unfair!" Dillon says. "Why should the government have all the cool stuff?"

"Don't get me started," I say.

"You always say that."

He drops me off at the office, then drives Sophie home.

You know that feeling you get when you unlock the front door to your house and *feel* something's wrong? In my case it's the front door of my office suite.

Maybe it's a scent. Maybe it's intuition. Maybe it's nothing. But *feels* like someone has been here since Dillon and I left earlier this morning. The feeling's so strong I consider walking right back out the door and waiting for Dillon.

Except that Dillon won't be back for at least twenty minutes.

And there's this: I have a gun.

I walk through the reception area, past the perpetually vacant reception desk, and get the distinct feeling someone not only entered the office after we left, but they're still *here*. To make matters worse, I hear sounds of activity coming from my office.

This can't be good.

I quietly place my handbag on the floor, remove my gun. Creep down the hall, past Dillon's office, the supply room, the break room, the bathroom. My office door is closed, as it should be.

There it is again!

And again.

The unmistakable sound of someone conducting a noisy search.

I pause, gun in hand, take a deep breath, silently turn the door handle with my free hand. I plan to push the door open while screaming, "*Hands in the air, asshole!*"

And shoot if I must.

That's the plan.

But while executing it, I fail to remember my office door doesn't push inward. It pulls outward. So when I push, nothing happens. But when I yell, "*Hands in the air, asshole!*" Someone screams inside, and—I don't mean to, but I—well, I discharge my handgun.

The screaming continues, so at least I didn't kill anyone. When it stops, I pull the door open, ready to shoot again.

It's a woman.

A redhead.

"Don't shoot!" she screams.

She's practically naked, covered only by the type of gown you might find in a hospital, tied at the neck, wide open in the back. The front of her body is pressed tightly against the wall, as if she's trying to blend with the drywall.

Except that she can't, because, like I said, she's a redhead.

That is not to say she has red hair.

In fact, she has no hair at all. On her head, anyway.

What I'm saying, her head is, quite literally, painted red. From the base of her neck to the top of her hairless scalp.

What else?

She's shapely.

I can't tell her age from this angle, but I can tell you she has a remarkable ass.

What makes it remarkable?

Her tattoos.

She has two.

One on each cheek.

Left cheek says *If I'm drunk....* Right cheek says, *Flip me over!*

"What the hell are you doing in my office?" I say.

"Looking for drugs."

"Who the fuck *are* you?"

"I'm Fanny, your receptionist."

"*What?*" Oh, *please no!* I'm aware my mouth has dropped open, but I let it hang that way. I flat don't care.

She turns to face me. "You're Dani."

It takes me a moment to form words with my mouth. I have to close it first. Eventually I say, "Why are you dressed like that?"

She moves away from the wall and I see she's hooked up to an IV stand. It has two hooks at the top to hold some sort of infusion solution that's being gravity-dripped into her wrist.

I point. "What's that?"

"Just a saline drip. No big deal. I just have to make sure the bag remains twenty-seven inches above my heart."

"Why's that?"

"Could you put the gun down, Sugar? I nearly shit myself when you tried to shoot me."

I look at the floor beneath her.

"Your carpet's safe," she says. "It's an expression, Sugar. Relax. Put the gun down, okay?"

I lower the gun.

She says, "According to the emergency room nurse, the infusion pressure's fifty mmHg at twenty-seven inches above the heart. At fifty-four inches, it's double."

"I don't understand."

"Neither do I, Sugar, but it's not as important as getting your envelopes pasted, right?"

"It sounds terribly important," I say, looking nervously at the needle in her vein, and the tube that's running red.

She follows my gaze and says, "I'll need to re-inject myself. I'll go outdoors so I won't bleed on your carpet."

"You shouldn't change that IV by yourself!"

"Don't you worry your pretty little head about it, Sugar. Last time this happened I wound up with subcutaneous crepitation. You'll hope that happens to me again, because it's fun. When air or gas gets trapped under my skin it'll feel like you're touching Rice Krispies."

"You need a doctor," I say.

"Don't be silly! I've already lived through the worst of it. These doctors and nurses are so full of themselves. Of course, their attitude is all, *"Don't you dare leave the ICU! You're taking your life in your hands!"* But then I explain how important these envelopes are to you, and—"

"Look, I feel terrible about that," I say. "And those awful texts I sent?"

"Don't give it a second thought. You have every right to expect a full day's work for a day's pay. And anyway, you know how it is with those doctors and nurses. They're just covering their asses. Speaking of which, how'd you like the tattoos on my butt?"

"Uh...I didn't mean to stare."

"That's okay, Sugar. You're not the first to enjoy the view. If you're ever in Soho, at Billy Bikers, check out the men's room wall, above the urinal. They've immortalized me. Framed photograph taken by Billy himelf."

"Why are you here?" I say.

"You told me to get my ass to work or you'd fire me. I can't afford to lose my hospitalization."

"You've got hospitalization?"

"Of course. So do you and Dillon! I'll get you a copy of the booklet that explains the benefits."

"How did you—I mean, how could you possibly sign us up for group hospitalization?"

"Can I be completely honest? I forged some documents, signed some checks."

"Who gave you check-signing privileges?"

She gives me a look. "Why, *you* did, Sugar."

"I don't think so."

"No? Well, hell, I probably forged your signature for that, too. Couldn't sign up for insurance without writing a check, after all. But no harm, no foul. I'm as honest as the day is long. Good thing, right?"

"Why are you looking for drugs in my office?"

"I couldn't go to the pharmacy dressed like this, could I?"

"I don't understand."

"I was looking for a prescription bottle. If you had one I could call the pharmacy, give them this scrip, maybe have them deliver my meds here."

"The pharmacy wouldn't fill your prescription under my name."

"Sure they would!"

"How's that possible?"

"I used your name when I checked into the hospital."

I frown.

"What's wrong?" she says.

"I'm sorry, Fanny, but this isn't working out. I'm going to have to let you go."

"Don't be silly!"

"I'm completely serious, Fanny. While I'm sympathetic to your unnamed illness, you're clearly a scam artist."

"In certain circles I'm known as a Nordic Princess, and a key member of the IVBF."

"What's that, a shoe store in Kettledrum, Illinois?"

"I can't say, never having visited the mythical kingdom of Kettledrum, where you might be town mayor," Fanny says. "But the IVBF *I'm* referring to is the International Virgin Boat Festival."

"We're getting off topic again."

"Here's a topic. You shot me with a handgun."

"Shot *at* you."

"In Minnesota, they call that attempted murder. Check the State Criminal Code of 1963, Section Number 609."

"We're not in Minnesota. And anyway, I thought you broke into my office."

"That's not going to play well with the police. They might wonder what sort of employer forces dying women in hospital gowns to come in and paste envelopes while hooked to IVs. Not to mention discharging a deadly weapon in the workplace. Check California Penal Code Section 12031 for reference."

"I'll take my chances. And by the way, we're in Tennessee, not Minnesota or California."

"I only know the statutes from places I've been arrested. But I'm confident with the possible exception of Texas, it's illegal to use your employees for target practice."

"Like I say, I'm willing to take my chances."

"Why, because I've got a blue tongue?"

"No, of *course* not! It's because—Wait. You've got a blue tongue?"

She sticks it out.

"Oh, *Jesus!*" I shout, covering my eyes. It's not only bright blue, but forked. I gag, and throw up in my mouth.

"You okay, Sugar?"

"You had your *tongue* split? *Completely?* On *purpose?*"

"Cleaved, Sugar. We call it cleaved."

I briefly wonder who she means by "we," but remember Donovan Creed, once said, "Don't ask questions unless you're prepared to hear the answer."

I'm not prepared for Fanny's answer. I don't want to know who *else* has their tongues cleaved all the way to their throats. But I'm curious why *she* does.

"Why would you *do* that, Fanny?"

She winks. "Ask my boyfriends."

"That will never happen."

"You know who else has a blue tongue?"

"No, and please don't tell me. I truly don't—"

"Bears."

"Excuse me?"

"My spiritual advisor says I'm directly descended from the union of a bear and a human."

The more she speaks the crazier she seems. I just want her out of here.

Still, I have to ask, "Which gender was the human?"

"Does it matter?"

"Not really, I suppose. Since the whole notion's preposterous."

"You wouldn't say that if you saw how much body hair I remove each week with my weed whacker."

I say, "Fanny, I'm sure you're a nice person and all, but you simply can't work here anymore. Surely you understand my position. You've forged legal documents, stolen money, and committed insurance fraud."

"You make it sound like a bad thing! Look, if something happened to poor Dillon, how would he be able to pay his medical bills? Surely you intended to provide him with hospitalization at some point."

"Well, of course. At some point."

"And you'd extend that coverage to your other employees, such as your devoted receptionist, right? I mean, you have to cover *all* your employees in order to qualify for group health insurance."

"Well..."

"You know what I think? I think you intended to provide coverage for Dillon, but never got around to it."

"Yes, but—"

"I just did what you intended to do. And now we've all got coverage."

"I can appreciate what you tried to do. It's not just the insurance, or the checks. It's *you*, Fanny."

"What about me?"

"I need a nice, quiet, prim and proper receptionist, who shows up every day and does only what I ask her to do. Someone who looks and dresses normally, who takes calls, schedules appointments, and—"

"Stop! You're making my ears scream! What you need is someone who looks at things differently. Someone who sees things others don't. Ask Dillon what he thinks of me."

"Dillon's eighteen. He hired you because of your boobs."

She smiles "You like them?"

"I don't know anything about them."

"Would you like to?"

"No. I'm just saying, he's an eighteen-year-old boy. He has no idea what criteria to look for in an ideal receptionist."

"Of course he does! He found *me*, didn't he? And anyway, he's here."

I turn around. "Where?"

"He's pulling into the parking lot right now."

"You can't possibly hear anything that far away."

"Shh!" she says. "Listen for the sound of the car door slamming shut."

"This is ridiculous."

She says, "There! Surely you heard *that!*"

"You're insane."

"You're telling me you can't hear him humming?"

This time she's gone too far. "Oh really? What tune?"

"Ravel's Bolero."

"Gotcha!"

"What's that mean?"

"Dillon's idea of classical music is Guns N' Roses."

"You got a problem with Guns N' Roses?"

"No, it's just—"

Dillon opens the door to the office, enters, walks through the reception area, down the hall toward us, humming Ravel's Bolero.

"Where did you hear that tune you're humming?" I demand.

"Fanny sent me a mix."

Fanny says, "The title hooked him."

"What, Bolero?"

"No," Fanny says, "The mix title. My song list. I call it—"

"—Stop! I don't want to know. You're trying to suck me into your vortex again."

Dillon says, "You look great, Fanny! How are you feeling?"

She smiles. "I've seen better days. And worse ones, too."

"Dani's having a bad day, too," he says. "We stole some cell phones hoping to find naked pictures of a girl, but they didn't have any."

"I know some great porn sites."

"Me, too. But this was a client. Something happened to her, but we can't prove it."

"Story of my life," she says. "By the way, Dani just fired me."

"Don't worry. She fires me all the time. You probably just got off on the wrong foot. Like I said, she's had a bad day. Still, I'm sorry she made you come to work like this."

"That's okay. I've been meaning to meet her for a long time."

"I'm right here in the room," I say.

"You should be in bed, Fanny," Dillon says.

"If I had a bedroom like the one on her computer, I'd never go outside."

I say, "What are you talking about?"

"The photos on your computer. Who's bedroom is that?"

"What the hell were you doing looking at my computer? You're out of line! That's completely unacceptable!"

Dillon says, "It's Kelli Underhill's bedroom."

"The girl who had the slumber party?"

"Uh huh."

133

"Well, whoever put the surveillance equipment in there did a helluva good job."

She turns to leave.

Dillon and I look at each other.

Surveillance equipment?

"Wait!" I say.

Chapter 25

Riley was right about the first four photos Dillon took of Kelli's bedroom using the camera's built-in flash.

"The flash makes 'em pop out like cold air on a warm nipple," Fanny says.

"Makes *what* pop out?" I ask.

She points to an area on the right side of the photo. "Right here. See that tiny light burst?"

"Yes."

"That's light, reflecting off a miniature camera lens. And see this one up here?"

"Yes?"

"That's another one."

"You're certain?"

"Of course. I used to install surveillance equipment for the CIA."

"I seriously doubt that."

"You can call and ask them. Central Insurance Agency. Two-forty Eddington Street, Montpelier, Vermont."

"Oh."

"Want their number?"

"No. But if you're right about the cameras—"

"Yes?"

"You can keep your job."

"Oh, goody."

"For now."

"How about a raise?"

"Don't press your luck."

"What if I tell you something else?"

"Like what?"

"Like—what's your client's name?"

"Riley Freeman."

"What if I told you these cameras have nothing to do with Riley?"

"What do you mean? They have *everything* to do with her."

"You're focusing on your case."

"That's my job."

"I agree. Which is why you need me."

"I'm waiting," I say.

"You're not seeing the bigger picture. There's more going on here."

"Tell me."

"This isn't the work of teenagers." Fanny says.

"No?"

"This is a professional installation. It took time. My guess, these cameras have been in place for a long time."

"What, exactly are you saying?"

"Someone's been spying on Kelli. And probably for a long time. You might find a video of Riley Freeman being assaulted, but Kelli's a victim, too."

I point at one of the photos. "This camera's directly above Kelli's bed?"

"Sure is."

"And this one covers her dressing area."

"Yup."

Dillon and I look at each other.

He shrugs.

I say, "How big a raise were you looking for?"

Chapter 26

At ten this morning, Riley shocked me with a question. At four-fifteen she makes a comment that knocks me for a loop.

"What do you *mean* you want to drop the case?"

"I'm sorry, Ms. Ripper. I'll find a way to pay you for your time. It's just that I can't do this."

"You owe me nothing, Riley. I haven't been charging you. But we have to see it through."

"I can't."

"Why not?"

"Kelli's my friend. If you tell the police about those videos, it could ruin her life."

"Riley, after all we've been through, surely you want to know what happened."

"Yes, of course."

"If there's a video, and it shows something happened to you, we have a responsibility to talk to the police."

"But what if there are videos of Kelli?"

"The police should know about that, too."

She goes quiet a minute.

I say, "You think she already knows?"

"What? No, of course not!"

"Any idea why she hates her stepfather?"

Riley stares straight ahead. "Please don't do this."

I say, "He keeps his bedroom door locked at all times, won't let anyone inside."

Riley says nothing.

"Look," I say. "It's just me and you. Please, honey. Tell me what you know."

She continues staring straight ahead a long time. Then says, "Promise you won't tell?"

"I promise."

"He raped her."

Chapter 27

"When did this happen?"

"Last summer."

"Kelli's stepfather raped her?"

"Yes."

"Who knows about this?"

"Me, Kelli, Mitch...I don't know if Kelli told anyone else. But Parker knows."

"Parker Page? Your best friend?"

Riley nods. "I told Parker about it a few months ago. She and Kelli were having a feud, and Parker kept treating her like shit."

"Does Lydia know?"

"Absolutely not."

"How can Kelli keep such a huge secret from her mother?"

"He threw himself on his knees and begged her forgiveness. Said he was drunk, under a lot of pressure in his job. He sobbed. Begged her not to tell her mom or anyone else. Kelli keeps thinking she must have done something wrong. That it's her fault, somehow."

"Except that he's spying on her."

"*If* he is."

"Has he touched her since?"

"No."

I think a minute. Then say, "You're positive she doesn't know about the cameras?"

Riley's eyes flash with sudden anger. "What are you saying? That my friend is *performing* for that psychopath?"

"No, of course not! You just made it sound like she's forgiven him to some extent. And has accepted part of the blame, which, by the way, is exactly how victims typically respond to this type of situation. But the bottom line is, she's keeping his secret."

"So?"

"You told me she hates Mitch. I was just wondering if, after being raped, she found out about the cameras."

"You need an additional excuse for why she hates her stepfather? She's fearful in her own home. Terrified when he's in town."

"Why do Kelli's parents sleep in separate bedrooms?"

"She caught him cheating on her."

"With whom, do you know?"

"He cheats a lot, Kelli says. Both locally and out of town, according to her mom."

"Why does she stay with him?"

"Money."

"I thought he was loaded. Wouldn't she do well in a divorce?"

"They have a pre-nup. And Kelli thinks most of his assets are hidden overseas."

"Which is why he travels so much?"

"I don't know. Maybe."

I shake my head. "That's why Kelli hasn't told her mom about the rape."

"Exactly. It's bad enough your stepfather rapes you. But it's even worse if you wind up homeless because of it."

"Is there a way we can get Kelli's mom out of the house so we can search Mitch's room?"

"How much time would you need?"

"As much as we can get."

She says, "You've taken a lot of chances, telling me about breaking into Kelli's house, searching her bedroom, stealing Ethan and Ronnie's phones. And now you're planning to break into Mitch's room."

"Not a smart way to do business, is it?"

"You could get into a lot of trouble."

"Are you planning to turn me in?"

"No. You're doing all this for me. You won't even let me pay you for your time."

"I'd break every law on the books to stop a predator."

"It's not that I'm ungrateful," she says. "But I'm planning to major in criminal justice, remember?"

"How can you have justice without evidence?"

She squeezes her eyes shut and winces, as if my words were live bees, stuck in her head.

Undaunted, I say, "So what do you think? Can Dillon and I get inside Kelli's house?"

"We'd have to tell Kelli about the cameras. If there are videos, I doubt she'd want Dillon looking at them. And certainly not the police."

"What about me?"

"The reason I chose you is because you've been through this before. Kelli might be okay with letting you see them. But definitely not Dillon, or the strange lady out front."

"Fanny?"

"That's her name?"

"Uh huh. She's the one who saw the light reflecting off the camera lenses in the photos."

"She works for you?"

"It's a long story."

"Is that actual paint on her head?"

"I think so. It seems too vivid for a tattoo. On the other hand, you'd expect paint to flake at some point."

"Did someone do that to her?"

"Far as I know, she did it to herself."

"Why?"

"Beats me."

"You never thought to ask? That would have been my first question during the interview process."

"Unfortunately, I wasn't there. But we can ask her, if you like. She's also got a cleaved blue tongue."

"What?"

"And tattoos on her butt."

"Eew. I hope she's a great receptionist."

"Jury's still out on that."

"Why is she in a hospital gown, hooked up to an IV?"

"It's a long story."

She pauses a moment, then says, "If Mitch made a video of me, I wouldn't want Dillon or Fanny to see it."

"No problem."

Riley's phone makes a sudden buzz.

"Text message," she says. She presses a button. "It's my mom. She's actually shopping at the mall and wants to know where I am. I better get going."

"Can I give you a ride?"

"That would be great."

As we walk through the reception area I notice Riley can't take her eyes off Fanny. I say, "Fanny, you never told me why you painted your entire head bright red."

"The Chiefs came to town last month."

"You're a Chiefs fan?"

"No."

Riley and I look at each other.

"Thanks for clearing that up," I say. "By the way, your tube's backing up with blood again."

She looks at it and frowns. Then looks at her wrist, touches it, and grins. "It's Rice Krispy time!" she shouts.

In the car, heading to the mall, I ask Riley if she thinks we can get Kelli on board.

"I don't know. Maybe. Right now, Lydia doesn't want Kelli talking to me."

"Because of me?"

"Yes. She's seriously considering a lawsuit against you for defamation of character. She's waiting on Mitch to come home before making the decision. Also, remember, Kelli doesn't know Dillon broke into her house and took pictures of her bedroom. That's going to creep her out."

"Maybe you can omit that part."

"I can try, I guess."

"Dillon's breaking in may have solved the whole case. It led us to finding the cameras. What if you tell Kelli we think Mitch made videos, and tell her she can have all of them except yours, and she can make her own decision about what she wants to do with them?"

"She might go for that, but only if I promise not to tell the police. If we take my video to the police, it automatically puts her in the middle of the circus. And if she does decide to tell her mom about the rape and the videos, and her mom goes to the police, won't there be a question about how she got the tapes? Couldn't Mitch's lawyers say the evidence is tainted or something?"

"I don't know. What if Kelli invites us in the house and says Mitch's door is stuck, and asks if there's anything we can do to help unstick it? When we get it open, maybe she looks around and says, 'Wow, look at all these video cards! I wonder if my prom pictures are on one of them! Can you guys help me look?'"

Riley shakes her head. "That's pretty lame."

"True. But I think the first step is to get in Mitch's room and photograph and video it exactly as we find it. Then, if there are any videos, we can check them out now, and decide what to do about them later."

Riley says, "In other words, we don't have to 'discover' them the same day we find them."

"Exactly."

"We'll have to do it soon," she says, "because Mitch is coming back tomorrow afternoon."

"Can you call Kelli and ask her?"

"I need to talk to her in person."

"Will her mom let her talk to you?"

"I think so. If I tell Kelli we've dropped the investigation, I'll be Lydia's best friend again."

"Are we dropping the investigation, Riley?"

"Yes."

"I think it's a bad idea. Ethan and Mitch are predators. We need to make them stop."

"I'm a junior in high school, Ms. Ripper. I don't want the whole world knowing about this."

"I understand how you feel. You know I do."

"I *do* know. But I'm just trying to survive high school and get into an Ivy League college."

"Please don't let them get away with this, Riley."

She smiles. "Let's do what you said. Take it one step at a time. Let's see if there's a video. If there is, let's see what it shows. If it's really bad, if I get really outraged, I can always re-open the investigation, right?"

"Yes, absolutely."

"Then let's approach it that way. In the meantime I can tell Kelli we've dropped the investigation because you're afraid of the lawsuit."

"Sounds good."

I notice Riley has dropped the whole "yes ma'am, no ma'am" politeness, now that she's fired me from the investigation.

I'm pleased.

Makes me feel like an old friend instead of an old lady.

Four hours later, Riley calls and says, "I spoke to Kelli. I've got good news and bad news."

Chapter 28

"Give me the bad news first," I say.

"Kelli went ballistic," Riley says.

"When you told her about the videos?"

"Yes."

"What did she do?"

"Kicked his door down and searched the room."

"Were you with her?"

"I was, yes."

"What's the good news?"

"We found them."

"The videos?"

"Yes. They're on CDs."

"Have you seen them?"

"No. I mean, we started watching one that showed Kelli getting dressed for school."

"Well, that's enough to put the bastard away right there."

"Probably. But there's more bad news."

"What else could possibly go wrong?"

"Kelli's mom has the CDs."

"She—*what?* What does that *mean?*"

"She caught us in Mitch's room, watching the video. When Kelli told her what happened, Lydia became furious. But she was furious with Kelli, not Mitch. They had a huge fight, and Lydia slapped her several times and grounded her. Then she started yelling at me, and said she was going to sue me."

"She can't sue you."

"I know. But she's really angry."

"We need to get a court order to confiscate those CDs."

"It's too late. She put them in a plastic trash bag, put me in her car and cussed me out all the way home. Then she drove away with the bag full of CDs."

"Damn it! Where was she going?"

"I don't know."

"What did she say?"

"She was really upset. She kept crying and yelling. Said she came upstairs because she knew I was up to something. She accused me of trying to ruin her life."

"What did she say about the CDs?"

"That she didn't care what was on them, she was going to destroy the evidence. No one was going to accuse her of providing an unsafe atmosphere for children. She said if I ever tell anyone about the CDs she and Kelli would deny it, and they'd sue me for slander."

"Have you spoken to Kelli since it happened?"

"Yes. And she's upset, too."

"What did *she* say?"

"She can't believe her mom's protecting Mitch after videotaping her, and seeing her naked all this time. She's embarrassed, humiliated, and angry. She can't believe her mom would take his side."

"Would she testify against her mom?"

"I doubt it. They're pretty close when they're not fighting."

Damn it, damn it, damn it!

"Okay," I say. "Let's see what we can salvage from this. Were you able to figure out what triggered the cameras?"

"What do you mean?"

"Did they run twenty-four hours a day, or just at certain times, or was there something specific that made them turn on and off?"

She doesn't answer right away, so I add, "Some cameras and voice recorders detect sound or motion. Some come on when it's dark and go off when it's light. Some—"

"The lights."

"Say again?"

"The camera starts recording when Kelli's bedroom lights are on. She has a lamp by her bed, and a switch on the wall where you enter the room. Both lights control the cameras. When the lights are on, the cameras record. When they're turned off, the filming stops."

"Oh. My. God!" I say.

"What's wrong?"

"Was the system still recording when you went in Mitch's room?"

"Yes."

I feel sick to my stomach.

"What's wrong?" she repeats.

"Dillon turned the lights on in Kelli's room to take pictures. He'll be on one of the videos. Unless it erased. Wait. Come to think of it, the system probably taped over your video and Dillon's."

"What do you mean?"

"Those CDs are probably only what, two hours each? Even if he used a really slow setting, each disk wouldn't hold more than six hours, max. And Mitch hasn't been there to change them for a whole week. The CD he put in the system last week has probably been re-recorded a half-dozen times by now."

"So even if we had the CDs, they probably wouldn't show what happened to me?"

"Probably not."

She sighs. "Ready to give up, yet?"

"No, never."

"What's left?"

"Several things. One, if we can keep Lydia from destroying the CDs, maybe she'll come to her senses and call the police to report her husband. That might give us leverage to open an investigation to a possible assault on you last Saturday night. Two, maybe you could get Kelli to call the police. If they go to her house right now, they'll be able to see the surveillance equipment, see how it works, and that will open everything up. From there, we might have leverage for the police to contact all the boys who were at the house that night. They'll get someone to talk about the photos Ethan and Ronnie took, and about what they told the others after it happened."

"But they said I woke up and was all over them."

"The photos prove it didn't go down that way."

"There *are* no photos, Ms. Ripper."

"Probably not. But the boys can testify to the photos they *saw*. Before Ethan's father had them erased."

"What good will all this do?"

"It will get Mitch off the streets and into prison, where he belongs. It will put Ethan's father out of business for tampering with evidence of a sex crime. It will lay the ground work for a civil suit against Ethan and Ronnie."

"But they're minors."

"Ethan's a predator. At the very least, we can make the police aware of the fact."

She pauses. "This has become very personal for you."

"Yes."

"I think we should let it go."

"No. You deserve justice, Riley. There are other things we could do."

"Like what?"

"You could still go to the police."

"And say what?"

"Exactly what you said to me. About what you think happened. You can tell them about the picture Rick Hooper bought from Nathan Cain. That puts Nathan right in the middle of it. The police are good at intimidating teenagers. He'll roll over on Ethan and Ronnie. I guarantee it."

"It's all hearsay," she says, sounding mature beyond her years. "To an attorney the photo shows a girl sleeping on a bed in her pajamas. And after making all those threats to Nathan, they'll go to Rick Hooper and find out about you and Dillon, and how you obtained the evidence, and that whole can of worms will be open. How would I feel if, because of me, you lost your license? Or if Dillon gets arrested for breaking and entering? Plus, Ethan and Ronnie are juveniles. They'll probably get their hand slapped, at worst. And everyone will talk about me, and I'll be a social pariah. It's just not worth it."

I sigh, thinking Riley Freeman, at seventeen years of age, might be twice as smart as me.

"Can we at least try to get Kelli to call the police? She shouldn't have to be in the house with that man. And honestly, Riley, he needs to be put away."

"She's not going to do that, Ms. Ripper. She's just not."

"Can I at least call her on the phone? I'd like to—"

My phone's being called. I check caller ID.

"Riley, can I put you on hold a second? Rick Hooper's trying to call me."

"Okay."

I click Rick's call through. "What's up, Rick?"

"I feel badly for what happened the other day. How we left things."

"It's okay, Rick."

"The first time we met, you walked away thinking I was a nice guy. The second time, I disappointed you."

I can't believe I'm having to deal with this right now.

"Truly, Rick, it's okay. You're a guy who's never been kissed. Never seen a girl naked, except for porn sites."

"Porn sites?"

"Don't lie in the middle of your apology."

"Okay."

"You had a chance to see the homecoming queen naked. I get it."

"Homecoming queen?"

"Figure of speech."

"Oh. Right."

"You're forgiven. You're still a nice guy. Just a little more human than I originally thought. And that's probably a good thing."

"Thanks, Dani."

"My pleasure."

I take a deep breath and say, "Was there anything else?"

"Yes. The main reason I called."

"Which is?"

"You said to let you know if anything changed. Or if there were any new developments. Something like that. I can't remember your exact words."

"And has it?"

"Huh?"

"Has anything changed or happened? Have there been any new developments I should know about?"

"There is one thing."

"What's that?"

"The nude photos of Riley just hit the internet."

Chapter 29

A lot happens in a short period of time. First, I break the news to Riley.

"How bad is it?" she says.

"I'd rather not describe it to you over the phone. Can I come to your house?"

"Why?"

"I'd like to be there for you, when you see them for the first time. I've been through this. We can talk to your mom together, let her know what happened. It's time to get her involved."

"Ms. Ripper," she says. "Can I call you Dani?"

"Yes, of course."

"Everything's about to blow up now, isn't it?"

"Yes."

"Then I think we've hit the point where you and Dillon can't be involved."

"What do you mean?"

"You guys have broken numerous laws to help build this case. I'm incredibly grateful, but now that the photos are on the internet, the case will take on a life of its own. But if *you're* involved, the defense attorneys will drag you into it and distract the police, the attorneys, and the judge."

"What about Kelli?"

"What about her?"

"This can be an opportunity to put Mitch away."

"Kelli and her mom should be the ones to make that decision."

"Okay, fair enough. Are you sure *you'll* be okay?"

"I'll be fine. I'm a survivor. All week we knew this could happen, so it's not like a complete shock."

"It's going to be very difficult for you. I'd like to help if I can."

"You can help by sending me the link to the photos."

"Of course."

"Thank you. And Dani?"

"Yes?"

"I really do appreciate everything you've done for me, and all the time you put into this."

"I'm still here for you, Riley. If there's anything you need, anything at all, please let me know how I can help you."

"Thank you. I would like to clear one thing up, though."

"What's that?"

"When you said you've been through this, it's not exactly true. What you went through was *far* worse than what happened to me. But how would you feel if naked photos of you were released on the internet?"

"I'd feel awful. I can't imagine it."

"Try to."

"Excuse me?"

"Do you realize everyone who knows me will look at those photos? Guys I know, their little brothers, and possibly their fathers, and some of my teachers—will probably masturbate to my photos. I doubt you have any idea what that's going to be like for me. Not to mention, I'll have to see all these kids and teachers at school every day."

"I'm so sorry, Riley. I didn't mean to compare our situations."

"I know. I'm just saying..."

I sigh. "I'll send the link. And the offer to call me, see me, work with me—will always be open."

"Thank you."

I send her the link, tell her goodbye, and pray she'll be okay.

That was around eight-fifteen p.m.

By eleven, Riley has become the lead story on all local news channels. They're not mentioning her by name, but they're scrambling to piece her story together.

By noon, Saturday, it's all anyone in town is talking about.

By five o'clock, there's a new lead story.

Mitch Underhill has been found dead in his own home, the result of an apparent suicide.

156

Chapter 30

Saturday.

As expected, the media loves the story of "the seventeen-year-old female student from Carson Collegiate."

I turn my TV on in time to see the camera zooming in for a close up of our enthusiastic, but somber-faced local TV anchor, Gwen Jeffries, who says, "Channel eight has just learned the photos were taken after the seventeen-year-old female honor student passed out after an evening of binge drinking at the home of Mitchell and Lydia Underhill, on Carriage Town Park, here in Nashville.

"The student had been attending a slumber party a week ago today, with four other teenage girls at the Underhill residence.

"According to sources obtained by our news department, sometime before midnight the girls opened the door to a number of fellow male students. Two of the boys allegedly found the student passed out in an upstairs bedroom, removed her clothing, and photographed her. They sent the photos to fellow students, who apparently forwarded them to others.

"A week after the incident, an unknown person posted the photos to an internet porn site. The photos were removed by the owners of the site upon discovering the student was a minor, however, authorities have filed for an injunction against the site and charged the owners with violating the Child Protection and Obscenity Enforcement Act.

"School officials have asked the student to refrain from attending classes. According to sources related to the story, the student is currently on a suicide watch, under a doctor's care.

"In a related story, Mitchell Underhill was found dead in his bedroom this afternoon, around four p.m. Underhill, who owned the home where the slumber party took place, is the apparent victim of a self-inflicted gunshot wound. Police say no one has been charged in the shooting at this time, pending the results of an autopsy. Viewers having additional information about either of these incidents are being urged by police to call the number on our screen."

As the anchor moves on to other stories, I receive a phone call from the last person on earth who should be asking me for help.

"Ms. Ripper?" he says.

"Yes?"

"I'm Gavin Clark. I'm—"

"Ethan's father."

"Yes. I'm calling to ask if you'd consider meeting me for a candid discussion?"

Curiosity helps me resist the urge to blow my whistle in the mouthpiece.

"When and where?"

"My office? Tonight?"

"Tonight's fine, but I don't trust your office. How about mine?"

"Same issue. Would you consider my country club? I can get us a private room."

"I'd prefer my country club."

He pauses. "Very well. Which club is that?"

"Actually, I don't have a country club."

"Excuse me?"

"I only said that to impress you. I thought you'd decline."

He sighs. "I'll come to your office if you give me your word there will be no recording devices."

"You'll have to promise the same."

"Fine. When I get there, we can remove our shirts to prove we're not wearing a wire. That's a joke, by the way."

He's making a joke? He must have spoken to Allen Roemer, the Underhill's attorney.

A half hour later, Gavin Clark enters my reception area with two teenage boys. I recognize one of them.

"Hello, Ethan," I say.

"What happened to your face?" he says.

"I ran into a bore."

"You mean 'door,' right?" Gavin says.

"Nope."

He says, "It does look painful. Introduce yourself, Ronnie."

"I'm Ronnie English."

159

He moves toward me, to shake my hand.

"I don't shake hands," I say. "Nothing personal."

"Germophobe?" Gavin says.

"No. But my explanation might make you nervous. Why are the boys here?"

"I want to talk to you with them present. At some point, if you're interested, I'd like you to hear their side of the story."

I frown.

Gavin says, "I know what you're thinking, that they've been coached. But I'll ask them to tell you what they told me. I can't guarantee it's the truth, but I'd like your take on it."

"What exactly do you hope to gain?"

"In a perfect world? I'd like to hire you."

"To do what?"

"Advise my legal team, help us obtain additional information, allow us to benefit from the investigation you've already conducted."

"You don't see that as a conflict of interest?"

"Not really. From what I understand, you were never hired by Riley or her mother. You were simply trying to find out what, if anything, happened to her at the slumber party."

"The photos have answered that question."

He glares at the boys, then says, "The photos are damaging. But they don't prove molestation."

I laugh, derisively. "You've seen the photos?"

"Yes, of course."

"And you think they don't rise to the level of molestation?"

"*Proof* of molestation, Dani."

"Please tell me how you would explain them. In a courtroom."

"I'd argue the photos have been displayed in the wrong order."

I laugh.

He says, "Assume Riley was completely naked when the boys arrived. And yes, they wrongly photographed her. But they were simply photographing what they saw when they entered the room."

"You make it sound like a bird watching excursion."

He shrugs. "What do you expect? I'm an attorney."

"It's exactly what I expect. But please elaborate."

"If the boys found her naked, and proceeded to dress her, and photographed each stage, to prove they were dressing her, they actually did her a service."

I wish I could say I never wanted to hurt someone as badly as I want to hurt Gavin Clark at this moment, but sadly, that isn't true.

Which tells you a lot about my life.

I swallow my anger and say, "The photos show Ethan kissing her genitals. Would I be safe in assuming he was aiming for the top of her head and fell short?"

He smiles. "If I thought the photos conclusively showed him kissing her genitals, I'd be even more furious than I am. Which is plenty. But the photos don't necessarily show proper perspective. I've had them studied and analyzed by professional photographers and criminologists, and the experts' consensus is the shading, the lighting, the camera quality—all come into play and give the *impression* something happened, when in fact, it didn't. Perhaps an example might help you understand."

"By all means," I say.

"Have you ever seen the collections of internet photos that appear to show things you know are impossible? Like a lady on the beach holding the moon between her hands? Or the little girl with her mouth open, and it appears a jet is about to fly into it? Or the guy who appears to be diving head first into a giant glass bottle? These are examples of perspective."

"Call me optimistic," I say, "but I think your average judge can differentiate between photos that show a guy diving into a bottle and Ethan diving into a girl's muff."

"You're quite optimistic, if a bit crude. I like that about you."

"You tipped your hand just now," I say.

"How so?"

"You said you've had the photos studied and analyzed by professionals. And yet they've only been online a few hours. Could it be possible you saw the photos on the boys' cell phones prior to them being published on the internet?"

"Whether I did or didn't doesn't matter, from a legal standpoint. I'm part of their legal team, and have been retained to represent them."

"You don't have an obligation to report a crime?"

"You and I share the same obligation, Dani. Why haven't *you* reported a crime? Answer: because you've had no conclusive evidence a crime was committed."

"Until now. The pictures show a crime."

"If that's the case, I'm obligated to make any evidence in my possession available to opposing counsel during the discovery process."

I say, "You're right. I was never retained to help Riley. But I'm obviously on her side."

"Of course. However, I hope to—if not persuade you—at least get you to look at the case in a more objective manner."

"Fat chance."

"I understand," he says.

"Does that mean we're done here?"

"I hope not. Ideally, I'd like us to have a short discussion, tell you where I see this case going, maybe get your opinion about some possible alternative solutions to Riley's predicament."

"*Her* predicament?"

"The boys are juveniles, Dani. If they were a year older, she'd have their nuts in a vice, and it would serve them right."

"I can get a vice. Bring the boys back when they're eighteen and we'll try it out. I'm sure Riley will be glad to participate."

"Well, as I say, it would serve them right. But I also pointed out they're juveniles. As bad as this is, as disgusting as their behavior has been, you and I both know they're going to wind up with a sealed record, probation, and possible community service."

"I don't know that at all," I say.

"Well, I could be wrong. On the other hand, this isn't my first rodeo."

I pause a minute. Then say, "Do you have any daughters?"

He shakes his head. "No. And you might not believe this, but my heart goes out to Riley. I can't imagine how a young girl like that would have the strength to cope. I can tell you these boys are remorseful. But I'll also be the first to say they have no conception of what they've done. They're upset, of course. They've learned a lesson. But are they more upset over being caught than about what they did?"

He waves his hand. Then says, "I honestly can't say."

He sighs. "This whole incident has devastated me. You raise your children, you think you've done everything right, and then something like this happens."

"Gavin," I say. "Can you cut to the chase? What did you come here to say?"

"This case is going to receive national media attention, and locally the boys will be talked about for a while. But neither the victim, nor the accused, will be publicly named. The boys won't do any jail or prison time, nor will Riley be awarded monetary damages."

"That's outrageous. Surely the courts will make an exception. Her photos are all over the internet. They're all over the school. She's lost her privacy. Her dignity. She's been forced to drop out of school. You're saying the boys will never be *named?*"

"If that's true, I'll make it my life's work to see that justice is done."

Gavin shrugs. "If she were my daughter I'd be just as upset. But the law's the law, and the legal system is what it is. And if I may, I know you're quite upset about what happened, and your passion for the victim is admirable. But I'd be remiss if I didn't caution you about making statements like the one you just made, regarding your personal desire to see justice done. That kind of comment, and any actions that support it, could be considered harassment. We've already got one victim. Let's not make a bad situation worse."

I feel my face getting flushed, but they know better than to smirk.

I silently curse the legal system, until it dawns on me if he's so fucking smart, and so convinced Ethan's got nothing to worry about, why bother talking to me in the first place? There must be more. I will myself to calm down. Then ask, "What else have you got to say?"

"Have you spoken to Parker Page?"

"About what?"

"Her role in all of this."

"What are you talking about?"

Chapter 31

"Don't misunderstand," Gavin Clark says. I'm not trying to create a diversion, or shift the blame…"

He adds, "The boys are guilty."

"They're going to plead guilty?"

"Of course. How can they not?"

"I don't understand."

"We expect them to be charged with voyeurism."

"Try sexual assault, counselor."

"There was no penetration, Dani."

"What about oral penetration?"

"The photos don't support that charge from a legal standpoint. At most they'll be charged with sexual abuse. But we'll fight hard to prevent that, based on the quality of the photos, the issues with perspective, and so forth."

"So why are you here?"

"Despite the way I'm coming across to you at the moment, I feel sick about what happened to Riley. These boys have ruined her junior year of high school, made it impossible for her to return to Carson for her senior year. She'll probably have to complete high school out of state, and the effects of this could follow her for years. You of all people understand this."

"Your point?"

"I want to help."

"How?"

"How's your relationship with Riley?"

"We're cordial."

"Does she trust you?"

"As far as I know. Why?"

"It wouldn't be appropriate for me to approach Riley at this point."

"I agree."

He starts to say something, then says, "I hope you don't take this the wrong way, but as an attorney I have natural trust issues. Can we step into the hall so I can ask you a question?"

"How long will it take? I don't want these guys snooping around my office."

"Twelve seconds. Guys?" he says to Ethan and Ronnie, "Stay exactly where you are till I get back."

"Hang on a sec," I say. "I have trust issues of my own."

I walk to the front door, open it, look around. Then say, "Let's go."

"Uh...your purse?"

"I'm not leaving my handbag in a room with your son."

"Might I at least verify there's no recording device in it?"

I open my handbag, remove the gun, and watch everyone's eyes grow big. It strikes me I'm enjoying their reaction a bit too much. Maybe this is what the gun ownership experience is about for the wrong people. Gives them a feeling of power. Control. By simply pointing this gun at Ethan, for instance, I could humiliate him a thousand different ways.

I think about a few of them.

No doubt about it.

I shouldn't be allowed to own a gun.

I let Gavin look through my handbag. Then I drop my gun in it, hang it on my shoulder, and follow him into the hall.

After closing the door, he says, "I wonder if you'd consider approaching Riley. Informally, of course."

"On your behalf?"

He purses his lips. "I'd ask you to approach her in a general way, as if you'd spoken to me about the case, and it doesn't appear the boys are going to receive much of a punishment."

"Riley plans to major in criminal justice. She's a gifted student, an excellent researcher. In other words, she already has a good handle on the limitations of her case. But she's not out for revenge, like I would be. At least, that doesn't seem to be her focus. At this point she just wants her life back."

"What if she thought you could get her a private settlement?"

"In return for what?"

"Not pressing the D.A. to charge the boys with sexual assault. Allow them to plead guilty to a criminal charge of voyeurism."

"And their sentence?"

"We'd let the judge decide."

"What's the worst they could get?"

"A felony charge for the voyeurism, five years' probation. They'd have to undergo counseling and sex offender treatment, and perform a hundred hours of community service tied to the crime, somehow."

"Such as?"

"If it were up to me, I'd have them clean toilets at the women's prison."

"Can we photograph them doing that and put it on the internet?"

"Sadly, no. But I wish we could."

"What else?"

"They'd be under the supervision of the juvenile justice department."

"Which means what, exactly?"

"They'd have to report regularly, and stay out of trouble."

"Doesn't sound like much."

"It's not, unless they fuck up. If they fuck up in the slightest, the world would come crashing down on their shoulders."

"And after five years?"

"If they remain clean and learn their lesson? The criminal offense would be dropped to a misdemeanor, and the record would be expunged."

"That's it? That's the worst?"

"Doesn't seem right, does it?"

I frown. "No."

"A million dollars might make her feel better about things."

I give him a look. "Must be nice being able to toss a million dollars at an inconvenience."

"It wouldn't be *my* money, Dani. It would come directly from Ethan's trust fund. He needs to make restitution. It will help him realize poor choices have consequences."

"Like tampering with evidence?"

"What do you mean?"

"I have reason to suspect you removed the photos from Ethan and Ronnie's cell phones."

"You probably suspect that because someone removed their cell phones from their lockers yesterday morning."

"Surely not! Wouldn't that violate the upper school's honor code?"

He smiles. "Was it just a coincidence I saw you in the hallway wearing a wig and ball cap?"

"Me? You must be mistaken, counselor."

"I'd say that too. But minutes after I saw you, Ethan was surprised to find Ronnie's phone in his locker."

I frown. "Where was Ethan's phone?"

"In Ronnie's locker. You must have been moving so quickly you got them mixed up. By the way, Ethan and Ronnie never sent nude photos to the others, though apparently they sent a photo of Riley lying on the bed, fully clothed."

"Who put the photos on the website?"

"I don't want to accuse anyone. But I have a damn good idea."

"Tell me."

"I'll let the boys tell you when we're through here."

I realize we've been in the hall more than twelve seconds. I open the door to make sure the boys are where they should be.

They are.

170

I close the door again and say, "Is the million dollars a sincere offer? If she says yes, you'll find a way to make it happen before this goes any further?"

"Yes. But it needs to happen before the boys are formally charged."

"How long do they have?"

"Almost certainly one day. Possibly two. What do you say? Will you talk to her?"

"What else can you offer?"

"What do you suggest?"

"Take away Ethan's car. Put him on foot for a year."

He smiles. "Done. What else?"

"I want him castrated."

He frowns. "Will you approach Riley with the offer?"

"Yes. But I want to hear what Ethan and Ronnie have to say."

"Then let's do," he says.

Chapter 32

"Tell Ms. Ripper what you told me," Gavin says to his son. "And if you lied to me about a single detail, fix it now."

Ethan has lost his swagger.

Maybe it's an act, but if so, it's a good one. He seems humbled. His father is clearly furious with him, and disappointed, and that's got to be uncomfortable.

He starts with, "Ms. Ripper, first of all I'd like to apologize for my behavior earlier this week. I was showing off, trying to act cool. When you put me in my place, I felt humiliated. I lashed out. When you handled that, I pouted. That's what spoiled, rich kids—who are full of themselves— tend to do. I wish I could claim this was atypical behavior on my part, but that wouldn't be true. I hope to become a better person. This situation will probably help me in that regard."

No doubt about it, the kid's got style. It's going to make him an effective serial rapist someday. I can't help but think what an extremely credible witness he'd be, if not for the fact he's the perpetrator.

I say, "You don't owe me an apology, Ethan. Just tell me what you came to say."

"Off the record?"

"It's just us here. I'm not involved in the case."

He looks at his dad. Gavin nods.

"Kelli and I texted each other all afternoon. This was last Saturday. She kept telling me the girls were coming to her house for a sleepover, and I should stop by with some friends after her mom fell asleep. I was worried her mom would be pissed, but Kelli said her mom's been drinking lately, and taking sleeping pills at night. She said by eleven or so her mom would be practically catatonic.

"That night a bunch of us were riding around, showing off, when Kelli texted me that her mom was completely zonked. She said they were drinking and had the house to themselves. She told me which girls were there, and that Parker would be leaving at midnight."

I interrupt. "What time was that?"

"Shortly after eleven."

"And what time did you enter Kelli's home?"

"About ten minutes later."

That's earlier than Riley reported, but Riley admitted she was woozy at the time.

"Go on," I say.

"Kelli asked if we could bring some liquor, because she was afraid if we stole some from the liquor cabinet her mom would find out. So we brought a case of beer. When we got to Kelli's, she took us to the basement, and we all drank and kidded around. I asked where Riley was, and they all started in on me about how I've always had a crush on her. Around that time Parker went upstairs for a few minutes. I figured she went to get Riley to come join the party. When she came back down alone, she got my attention from the stairwell, and motioned for me to come over. I did, and Ronnie followed. She took us upstairs and said, "Your girlfriend's upstairs in Kelli's room, passed out."

"No way!" I said, because we all knew Riley doesn't drink.

"Ever?"

"Ever."

"I asked if she was okay, and she said, 'Come see.'"

"She led us up the back stairs and opened the door. We couldn't see much, because it was dark. She called Riley's name, but Riley didn't answer. Then she walked in the room and said, 'Check this out.'

"She used the flashlight app on her cell phone and led us to the bed. Then she slapped Riley's face lightly, then a little harder, and said, 'Riley, wake up!'"

I frown.

"Go on," I say.

"Parker said, 'This girl is bombed. You could do anything to her and she'd never know.' Then she laughed and said, 'Want to know a secret?' We said sure. She said, 'Promise you won't tell?' We promised. She said as a joke she pulled Riley's pants down and stuck a strawberry sticker on her twat."

He notices the look on my face and says, "Sorry for the language. Those were her words, not mine." Then he says, "We didn't believe her, so she said, 'Check this out.' She handed me her cell phone and told me to hold the light on

Riley. Then she lifted Riley's shirt up and showed us her boobs. We freaked out. She let us look for a few seconds, then pulled her shirt back down. Then she said, 'Truth or dare.' I said, "Dare." She said, 'Walk me out.'

"We walked out of the room with her, and she said, 'My mom will be here in fifteen minutes. Have fun with Sleeping Beauty.' I said, 'What's the dare?' She said, 'I dare you to take a picture of the sticker. But be quick. I can only keep the others busy till my mom gets here.'

"I said, 'What are you going to tell the others we're doing?' She said, 'I'll tell them you went out to the cars to look for more beer.'

"Then she turned the light on and walked away."

I say, "Then what?"

He says, "You know the rest."

I look at Gavin. He says, "What's your take?"

I look at Ronnie. "That's how you remember it?"

He nods.

"You're telling me her best friend set her up?"

Ronnie says, "It's not a good excuse. Parker didn't make us do anything. But yeah, she got us all hot and bothered, and we'd been drinking. Parker was Riley's best friend. We knew it wasn't right, but Parker made it seem almost okay to fool around with Riley, since she already stripped her and found the sticker."

"So you did."

"Yes, ma'am."

"So the first time the light went on is after all three of you walked out of the room?"

Ethan says, "Yes, ma'am."

175

"So you and Ronnie walked in, left the lights on, and closed the door?"

"Yes."

"Why didn't you turn off the lights?"

"We thought the whole thing might be a joke. We went in, looked in the closet and under the bed to see if anyone was hiding there. At first it was like one of those What Would You Do? situations. Plus, we wanted to see if we could catch Riley faking it. So we tried tickling her nose, and pushing her around on the bed. We said, 'Come on, Riley, quit faking. Open your eyes!' But she didn't. We pulled and pushed her some more and then it was almost like, 'Well, this will prove she's faking!' and we touched her inappropriately over her clothes. When she didn't respond, it was just so easy to look for the sticker Parker told us about. We took some pictures."

"Where are the pictures now?"

"We sent one to our friends, and erased the others."

Ethan notes the skeptical look on my face and says, "You don't believe me?"

"I'm still making up my mind. But I heard there's an app that would show any picture ever taken from your cell phone, even if you erased it. If the police downloaded that app on your phone, I should be able to find those photos, right?"

"I don't know," he says. "But these aren't the phones we used that night. After we sobered up we realized we could be in a shitload of trouble if Parker told anyone what happened. Ronnie and I erased all the texts and photos. The next day we bought new cell phones and had all our contacts and photos transferred to the new ones, except for the texts or photos from Saturday night. Then we smashed the old phones and threw the pieces in dumpsters."

This would explain why Riley's photos didn't show up on Ethan and Ronnie's cell phones. It would also prove Gavin didn't tamper with the cell phone evidence, although he probably directed them to destroy the old phones and purchase new ones.

I decide it's time to ask the obvious question.

Chapter 33

"If you erased all the photos, how did they manage to show up on the internet?"

Ethan and Ronnie look at Gavin. He says, "Don't state it as a fact. Just say what you think might have happened."

Ethan says, "We only sent the naked photos to one person. Parker Page. To prove we did the dare. I know it sounds stupid now, and I'm not making any excuses for our behavior. But that's how we justified it at the time. I asked Parker to erase the photos and get a new cell phone and she said she would. But maybe she didn't. Or maybe she did after posting the photos."

"How long were you in the room alone with Riley?"

"Two or three minutes each."

I almost missed the last part of the sentence, because Gavin screamed, "Don't answer that!" at the very moment Ethan was, in fact, answering. And had it not been such a startling event, I might have missed the importance of his final word.

He said, "*Each.*"

As in, they *each* spent two or three minutes alone with Riley.

Since Gavin was, and is still clearly upset by the answer, I take a moment to consider the full implication. And come up with this: the boys stripped Riley, took pictures of her, then split up. One must have guarded the door while the other...

I decide to go all in.

"You said you *each* spent two or three minutes alone with Riley?"

Ethan and Gavin say nothing. They're locked in a stare down, and Ethan's losing.

"Ronnie?" I say.

"*I didn't!*" he says.

Gavin says, "What Ethan meant to say is they spent two or three minutes alone in the room with her."

"He said *each.*"

"It was a word he used casually, one he wouldn't repeat in a courtroom, where every word of testimony is parsed. But I've heard this story numerous times, so let me clear things up. They each spent that much time alone with her, while together. In other words, neither of them left the room without the other. That's my understanding. Ethan? Ronnie? If I'm not completely accurate in making that statement, please correct me now."

They say nothing.

"So I've got the story right? You were both there at all times?"

They nod.

Vigorously.

Gavin went to a lot of trouble to make that clear, as he had to. But it's obvious the boys took turns with Riley. I shudder to think what that means.

Gavin allows his facial features to soften. Then shows me a practiced, lawyerly smile.

"Dani," he says, "we came here tonight for several reasons. Cross-examination isn't one of them. My son misspoke. He's nervous. Who wouldn't be?"

I decide to let it go.

For now.

But all I can think is how different things would be if Kelli and Riley could have found and preserved the video. What do they call it in the NFL? Conclusive video evidence? That tape would have given us...everything. It would have started the moment Parker left the room and turned on the lights.

I end the uncomfortable silence in the room by saying, "You're laying an awful lot of this on Parker."

Gavin says, "Quite true. That's why I asked if you'd spoken to her yet."

"I have not. Have you?"

"Yes."

"And?"

"She admitted everything."

Chapter 34

If I live to be a hundred, I doubt I'll ever be more surprised than I am this very moment. I hope I never hear anything that disgusts me more.

But I know better.

I'm in a sleazy business.

"How'd you get Parker to confess?" I ask.

Gavin says, "I put the fear of God in her."

I try to think of something to say, but my mind's going in a hundred directions at once. I think about the details Ethan provided. He liked Riley. That's something I didn't know. And since he liked her, it's natural he'd wonder where she was. He didn't get up and roam through the house looking for her, but it makes sense her best friend, Parker, would go fetch Riley back to the party. So he was looking for them to return. Which is why it makes sense he'd notice Parker returning alone. Of course he'd sneak over to the stairwell when Parker motioned him to come. She obviously had news she didn't want to share with the group. And it makes sense Ronnie followed him, because that's what Ronnie does.

He follows Ethan.

Not only do these details make sense, they fit the general timeline Riley provided.

Ethan's account answers some of the questions that have nagged me from the start. One, if Parker went looking for Riley before her mom came to get her, why wouldn't she check Kelli's bedroom? (She did). Two, what gave Ethan and Ronnie the courage to stay in the room with Riley all that time while more than a dozen kids were in the house? (Parker was running interference for them). Three, why didn't the rest of the group, especially Kelli, notice Ethan and Ronnie were missing the whole time they were gone? (Parker told them they were outside, searching the cars for more beer).

It all fits.

If Ethan's story is true, Parker's in it up to her eyeballs. According to him, Parker committed all the same crimes. Except there's no evidence of that. Parker didn't take any photos. Whatever she did wasn't witnessed by anyone else. Even if we had the video, it wouldn't show Parker's involvement, because according to Ethan, the lights in the room were off until just before the boys entered the room. Either Parker's the luckiest girl in the world, or...

Or she knew about the cameras in the room, and how they worked.

But how's that possible? Even Kelli didn't know about the cameras.

Riley was positive she turned the light on in Kelli's room that night, before going to use Kelli's bathroom. If she's right, someone had to turn off the light before Parker brought Ethan and Ronnie into Kelli's room. If Parker turned them off, was it before or after entering the room the first time? If after, the video would have shown whatever she might have done.

God, I wish I had that video!

I say, "Does anyone else know about Parker's role in all this?"

"We don't think so," Gavin says.

"Is her confession admissible?"

"Not even close."

"Why not?"

"I'd rather not go into details."

"What if you're asked by the court?"

"I'd say she came to my office, and this is what she told me."

In addition to putting the fear of God in her, Gavin must have paid her to confess. That doesn't make her confession false, but it makes it inadmissible. I don't know if Parker understands that, but her attorney would.

"Has Parker lawyered up yet?" I ask.

"Not to my knowledge."

"If she's charged, she'll probably deny everything she told you."

"I'm sure she will," Gavin says, "because her attorney will know there's absolutely no proof. It would come down to her word against Ethan's. And who's going to believe him?"

"So what's the value of her confession?"

"It helps me understand how my son could do something so...*vile*. I'm not condoning what he did. I'm just saying I understand. The boys fucked up. But they're boys. Yes, they did a terrible thing. But it's not the same as if they'd been prowling around the house, looking for Riley, only to find her passed out, and then making the conscious, independent decision to take advantage of her."

"I'm sorry," I say. "Can you explain to me how it's the slightest bit different? It seems to me when Parker walked away they *did* make the conscious, independent decision to molest her."

Gavin says, "I can see it from your viewpoint. I'm just saying the way it went down, it was a lot of temptation to put on two teenage boys after a night of drinking."

"None of which improves Riley's situation."

"Which is why I hope you'll approach her."

He hands me a piece of paper.

"What's this?"

"A nondisclosure and confidentiality agreement. It simply states that you agree to keep all dealings between you, me, and Riley, confidential. There are three copies. You can keep one and give one to Riley if you want."

I review the document, then sign all three copies, and keep one for myself. Then we all stand up. Before they have a chance to leave, there's a sharp knock at the door, and a giant space creature suddenly bursts in, holding a see-through plastic baggie containing a woman's soggy panties. He says, "I saw your light on as I was driving by. *Here!*"

"Eric?" I say.

He shoves the baggie in my hands and runs back out the door.

I frown, and drop the baggie on the reception desk.

The four of us stare at it in disbelief.

Gavin shakes his head and says, "This happens very rarely."

"What does?" I say.

"Every once in a while, when I'm overwhelmed, and think I'm in the world's most disgusting profession, something like this happens, and I thank God."

I frown.

They leave.

I take Erica's panties into the kitchen, spray the crotch, compare them to the other pair in the refrigerator.

Cobblestone's right. His wife is cheating on him.

Do I care?

Not really. Not now.

I bag them, tag them, put them in the fridge.

I'll care tomorrow. But right now, my heart aches for Riley.

So I call her.

Chapter 35

"How strong is the friendship between you and Parker?"

Riley answers, "Why would you ask me that?"

"I think it's about to be tested," I say.

"Why?"

"Can we meet?"

"When?"

"Right now?"

"Wow. I don't know. Things are crazy around here," she says.

"Your mom?"

"That's part of it. And a police detective wants to talk to me tomorrow."

"What time?"

"Afternoon."

"When did your mom find out?"

"An hour ago. When the news reporters showed up on our front lawn."

I feel badly for her. This part I've been through, more than once.

It's not pleasant.

"I'm sorry, Riley. That's awful. For both of you."

"I would've told her sooner, but I didn't think they'd identify me so quickly. She's devastated, of course. This is probably not a great time to meet with you."

"I have something important to tell you."

"About Parker?"

"That's part of it. I met with Ethan and Gavin Clark, and Ronnie."

She pauses. Then says, "I asked you to stop pursuing the case."

"They contacted *me*."

"But you haven't spoken to Parker."

"No, but she met with Gavin, and according to him, Parker admitted to being deeply involved in what happened to you Saturday night."

"Don't believe everything you hear. Parker's my best friend. On the other hand, Gavin Clark's a sleaze bucket who'd say anything."

"I'm glad to leave Parker out of it. But I do have important news."

"Can we discuss it on the phone?"

"No. And time's a major factor."

"It's pretty late. I doubt my mom will drive me there."

"I can come to you, but we need to talk privately, if possible."

"If you come to my house and park out front, we can talk in your car. Would that work?"

"I can be there in ten minutes."

"You know my address?"

"Please. I'm a private investigator."

"Most people have trouble finding my house the first try."

I start to say something clever, then realize I don't need to impress her. She's already fired me. And there's this: I don't know how to work my GPS.

"Give me the address," I say.

I pause. Then add, "And the directions."

Chapter 36

"There's one benefit to being a minor," Riley says.

"What's that?"

"The police forced the camera crews to leave."

"That's good news, at least."

I'm happy for her, but mildly surprised, because ten years ago the media hammered me after I escaped from Colin Tyler Hicks's basement. It got so bad Mom and I had to move away and change our names.

Riley says, "What's your big news?"

We're in my car, on the street in front of her house. Riley looks remarkably composed. If I didn't know better, I'd think it was just another day in her life.

"I heard you were under a doctor's care, on suicide watch."

"My mom just told the media that so they'd back off. I'm fine."

"You *look* fine," I say, "though I have no idea how you manage it."

"What's my alternative?" she says. "What's done is done. Time to move past it."

I shake my head in disbelief, and feel like I always do when I'm in Riley's presence: like I'm with someone who's in complete control. Indeed, now that I think about it, every setback we've faced bothered me more than her.

"You may be seventeen," I say, "but you're the most together person I've ever met. At any age."

She smiles. "I'm a duck."

I give her a curious look. "Care to elaborate?"

"When you see a duck in a pond, the part you see is peaceful, quiet, and serene. But under the surface, his legs are kicking away, churning water. That's me."

"Well, I'm impressed."

"Thanks," she says.

She looks at me, expectantly.

I say, "Okay. The reason I'm here, Gavin Clark brought Ethan and Ronnie to my office tonight. They told me their version of what happened."

"If I understood you correctly, they implicated Parker."

"In a major way. And Gavin said he met with her and she corroborated Ethan's story. Wait. Are you smiling?"

"I am."

"Why?"

"Because that's the story Ethan concocted to tell his dad. Parker rehearsed it with him, and when his dad met her, she managed to score ten grand from him to tell it."

I frown. "And you're okay with that?"

She shrugs. "What do I care? It has nothing to do with me."

"What if Parker has to testify?"

"Then she'll tell the truth. Ethan gave her the story, his dad paid her ten thousand dollars to repeat it."

"She took advantage of him."

"Not at all. Parker didn't make up the story, Ethan did. Parker didn't call Gavin to sell him a confession, he called her. She agreed to meet him. When she did, he yelled at her and threatened her. In the end he paid her money to tell him what he wanted to hear. Something that would make him feel better about his degenerate son. He probably doesn't believe it, but it gives him something to hang his hopes on."

I study her face. "Who *talks* like this?"

"What do you mean?"

"I know you're intelligent, but you sound like you're forty years old. Worldly beyond your years."

"Thanks. I think. But really, it's not that big a deal. I saw a girl on TV last night who wrote a complete opera that's going to be performed by a major symphony. You know how old she is? Seven! Imagine where *she'll* be when she's *my* age!"

"You called Parker right after we spoke."

"I did. So I could find out what you were talking about. In fact, she and I were still on the phone when you pulled up."

"And you're convinced she didn't do any of those things?"

"That's right. Plus, she didn't know about the sticker till Ethan concocted the story."

I shake my head. "I don't know, Riley. I know she's your friend, but she sounds a bit conniving to me."

She smiles. "We're *all* conniving, Dani."

She notes my confused expression and adds, "We're teenagers."

"Okay. So anyway, Gavin's concerned about the case."

"I don't blame him."

"Really? Because he makes it sound like you're going to come away with nothing. According to him, the maximum they'll get is probation, a hundred hours of community service, and in five years or less, their criminal records will be expunged."

"Which is it?"

"What do you mean?"

"On the one hand you say he's concerned about the case. On the other, you say he's got nothing to worry about. Which one's more likely to be accurate?"

"The first. He's worried."

"Has he instructed you to make me an offer?"

"How did you know?"

"Rich people always try to buy their way out of trouble. What's the offer?"

I look her in the eyes before responding, so I can enjoy her reaction. Then I say, "One million dollars. Cash."

"In return for what?"

I stare at her in disbelief. She didn't even flinch. I just offered a financially-strapped, seventeen-year-old girl a million dollars and she didn't bat an eye.

"Gavin's going to ask the court to limit the criminal charges to voyeurism. But he knows your attorney will want to add sexual assault."

"So if I can talk my attorney out of the sexual assault charge, Gavin will pay me a million dollars?"

"Yes. He says it's coming from Ethan's trust fund."

"He's assuming I'll jump at the offer, since I can't sue Ethan or Ronnie in civil court."

"Exactly. So, what do you think?"

She says, "I think the offer's a bit light."

"Excuse me?"

"Tell him I'll take five million. Nothing less."

My eyes grow wide.

She laughs. "I'm serious, Dani. Tell him he's got twenty-four hours to come up with the money."

After picking my jaw up from the floor I say, "Riley, I don't even know how that type of transaction would *work*."

"Remember the charity I told you about? The one I started last year? It's a small charity that helps underprivileged kids get scholarships to private schools. I've only raised a few thousand dollars so far, but it's a qualified charity. When Gavin's ready to make a contribution, I'll give you the details."

"Just to be clear: you don't want him to write *you* a check. You want him to make a five million dollar donation to your charity?"

"That's right."

I pause a moment, then say, "I'll deliver the news."

"You don't think he'll go for it, do you?" She says.

"Honestly? No."

She nods. Then says, "Do you have something to take notes with?"

"I do. Why?"

"I'm going to tell you a little story that will mean something to Gavin."

She waits for me to get a pen and notebook from my glove compartment, then says, "For years I've been doing odd jobs to make extra money. Like babysitting, assisting elderly people with chores, running errands for them, and so forth. A couple of years ago I was cleaning out an elderly lady's attic."

She pauses, then says, "Mona Elkins."

She waits till I write the name. Then says, "Before she retired, Mona used to be Allison Clark's personal assistant. Allison was Gavin's first wife, the one he married before the trophy one. I took care of Mona one summer, and over time, we bonded. One of my projects was cleaning out her attic. I did a box or two every day for two months. I meticulously went through every piece of paper, reviewed every item with her before putting it in the throw-away pile. At some point we realized I was attending the same school as her former employer's son, Ethan."

She waits for me to catch up. Then says, "Imagine my surprise the day I found two copies of Ethan's birth certificates among Mona's possessions."

I say, "Did you mean to use the plural?"

"Yes, absolutely."

"I don't understand."

"I didn't either, at first. So I asked Mona about it. And you know what she said?"

"What?"

"She said, 'Promise you won't tell?'"

Riley winks at me.

"What?"

"I promised I wouldn't tell."

I look at her.

She says, "Tell Gavin I've kept my promise to Mona. So far."

I frown. "You're not going to tell me what Mona said?"

"Not yet."

"Why?"

"I want you to be able to honestly say you don't know what I'm talking about."

"But Gavin will?"

"Gavin definitely will."

I sigh. "I'll deliver the news."

"Dani?"

"Yes?"

"He's paying you, right?"

"No. He offered to, but I declined."

"Why?"

"I told him I was on your side."

She smiles. "You're a good friend, but you should get something out of it."

"I just want your life to get better."

"When my charity gets going, I hope you'll let me hire you to do background screening on the applicants and their families."

"I'd like that. Thanks."

I laugh.

She says, "What's so funny?"

"Yesterday I offered *you* a job. Now you're offering *me* one."

"What a difference a day makes, right?"

Chapter 37

"Excuse me?" Gavin says. "She said no? She's turning down a million dollars? What the hell did she say, exactly?"

"She said a million dollars seemed light."

"*Light?* What the fuck does *that* mean?"

"She wants five million."

He laughs a full minute. Laughs so hard his body shakes. Laughs so hard he has to dab the tears from his eyes. When he finally stops laughing, he says, "There's got to be more, and I can't wait to hear it. What else did she say?"

This time I'm in Gavin's office. We're alone.

I say, "She told me a story."

"What story?"

"I can't do it justice, but I took notes."

I remove the notepad from my handbag and say, "She's been doing odd jobs for years. Mostly caring for the elderly, in their homes. Running errands, cleaning attics, and such. One summer she worked for a lady named Mona Elkins, who..."

Up till now, Gavin was semi-reclining in his chair, showing me an indulgent smile as he waited patiently for me to get to the point. Now his chair's upright. His smile a memory.

"I know that name," he says. "Mona Elkins." He furrows his brow. "How do I know that name?"

"Before retiring, she was your ex-wife's personal assistant."

Gavin's face moves from curious to concerned.

"And how does this happy coincidence affect Riley's case?"

"I honestly don't know. But she gave me a message for you, and said you'd understand."

He frowns deeply and says, "You're working for her now?"

"No."

He gives me a hard stare. "You're sure about that?"

"Quite sure."

"Do you *never* accept payment?"

"Not for these types of cases."

He says, "In that case I definitely want you on my payroll."

"That wouldn't feel right. I'd rather limit my role to go-between. Consider me the messenger."

"Suit yourself." He waves his hand through the air, indicating nothing in particular. "You don't want to get paid? Fine. Don't get paid. You're the messenger. Whatever." He takes a deep breath and says, "So...what's the message?"

"Riley was cleaning out Mona's attic. Said she went through each box meticulously, one piece of paper at a time. Said she found two copies of Ethan's birth certificates."

I pause to see what impact my words have on him, but his face remains unchanged. He's looking at me, waiting for me to continue.

"That's it," I say.

"Excuse me?"

"I asked if she meant to use the plural and she said yes, absolutely."

"Plural of what?"

"Birth certificates."

Like a long fuse on a bomb, it takes a moment before my words have the impact Riley anticipated.

Gavin jumps to his feet. Ten expletives jump with him and escape his mouth in such a hurry it sounds like he's speaking in tongues. He shakes his head and mutters and kicks his coffee table like an angry child. He walks to the floor-to-ceiling window and curses the skyline. Crosses the room and punches the wall.

"Riley Freeman's a fucking shakedown artist!" he yells. "A *blackmailer*! You *know* that now, right?"

I say nothing. Truth is, I like Riley even more than I dislike Gavin and his sleazy kid. *Why is that?* I wonder. *Am I too close to the situation?*

Probably.

Yes, Riley is suddenly seeking compensation, but does that make her a blackmailer? Seems to me she's learning how the system works and has decided to use it to her advantage. I mean, she certainly didn't *ask* to be molested. And she's clearly been sitting on this birth certificate thing for years. Whatever information she has, the idea of using it against Gavin never came up until he offered her cash. Had she planned to use it against Ethan all along, she would have told me about it days ago, when we learned he's the one who molested her.

But she didn't.

So I'm not comfortable calling her a blackmailer or shakedown artist. Is she shaking him down right now?

Yes. No doubt about it.

But it's an after-the-fact shakedown. Like the way she described Parker's situation. Ethan approached Parker first, then Gavin approached her. Is it possible *Gavin's* the one who concocted the story? Could he have told Ethan to spoon-feed the story to Parker, so he could get her to "confess" in a secret recording? And if so, why would Parker go along with it?

The easy answer's the photos.

Did Ethan send her nude photos of Riley? In his version, it would make sense that he did. In Parker's version, there would be no point.

It's pretty confusing.

Much as I hate to admit it, I believe Parker's lying. I think she was deeply involved in what happened to Riley. Not that I believe a hundred percent of Ethan's story, either. And now that I think about it, I have no way of knowing which parts of Ethan's story Parker "admitted" to, when confessing to Gavin.

My gut tells me this is what happened: Parker went searching for Riley and found her passed out in Kelli's room. She didn't strip her, or put a sticker on her private area, but I believe she went to the basement, got Ethan's attention, and took him and Ronnie upstairs. I believe she was semi-drunk, and goofing off, though I doubt she pulled up Riley's shirt to get the boys all "hot and bothered." But even if she did, I expect that's as far as she ever expected it to go, because at that point, her mom arrived. In Ethan's account, Parker said, "Have fun with Sleeping Beauty" just before leaving. I buy that. The phrase has a ring of truth to it.

To me.

But if she said it, I expect she was just kidding. I seriously doubt she dared them to strip Riley and take photos. I expect she left, assuming the boys would go back to the basement. If they sent her photos, I expect it was because they were drunk, and full of themselves. But I don't believe she posted them to the internet. More likely she forwarded them to someone, and that person posted them.

I briefly wonder if Riley herself might have posted them, to build the case.

Wouldn't that be something?

It would, except there's no way she would ever post nude photos of herself on a porn site. And if you think I'm wrong, consider how intelligent she is. Riley certainly knows how easy it would be for the police to find that type of evidence on her computer or cell phone.

There's a lot of "he said, she said" to this case, but the one point everyone agrees on is Riley was passed out and inappropriate things happened to her. And personally I'm convinced that Ethan and Ronnie went way beyond what they're willing to admit. Though I haven't said anything about it to Riley, I believe they took turns guarding the door.

Which means they took turns being alone with Riley.

Which might mean lots of things.

Was there penetration? If so, what type? Was there sufficient penetration to satisfy the legal definition of rape?

The police might be able to answer that question after running tests on the bedspread.

All these thoughts are going through my head while sitting in Gavin's office.

What's he doing in the meantime? Stomping back and forth from one side of his office to the other, with red-faced rage. He's muttering about his ex-wife, Allison, and her private secretary, Mona, and a dozen other things I can't make out.

He's in the midst of a full-blown temper tantrum.

"This is bullshit, Dani! *Bullshit!* I won't stand for it! That bitch has no clue who she's dealing with. No clue, whatsoever. I'll *fry* her ass! I can't *wait* to see her in court! Turn down a million *dollars?* From *me?* For *this* piece of shit case? Who the fuck does she think she is?"

It goes on like this for another five minutes. He's got himself so worked up I fear he'll suffer a stroke. Finally, he takes a seat at his desk and closes his eyes. He takes a deep breath and says, "I'm sorry, Dani. Sorry you had to see that. If this were simply a case of her going after me, things would be different. But she's going after my son, threatening to ruin his life."

Though I say nothing, I find it amazing he's able to reframe these events as Riley going after his son, trying to ruin his life. Did Riley invite Ethan to the party? No. Did she let him in the house? No. Did she flirt with him? Tease him? Lead him on in any way? No. Did she threaten anyone with this birth certificate thing or demand a cent before any of this happened? No. Gavin wants me to believe Ethan's the victim?

Unbelievable!

Ethan stripped an unconscious, underage girl. Molested her. Sexually abused her. Might have raped her.

But *he's* the victim?

I look at my handbag, on the floor, by my feet. This is a perfect example of why I shouldn't be allowed to carry a gun. Because if all this had happened to me, and I heard him talking this way, I'd blow this motherfucker away, right here, right now.

He says, "Do you have children?"

I shake my head, no.

"Well, someday, if you ever *do* have kids, you'll understand. You'll do what you can to protect them. This case is bullshit. She knows it, I know it."

He looks at me. "Even *you* know it."

What's that, asshole? Even I know it? Is that what you said?

What a condescending prick he is! I kick my handbag further away from my feet, so I'm not tempted to grab my gun.

He says, "She's got my ass in a sling and she knows it. She's going after my son. That's my weakness, and she knows it."

I'm steaming from all his comments, but like Riley's duck example, I'm trying not to show it. I'm keeping my true feelings underwater. But that doesn't mean I'm not going to enjoy twisting the knife a bit. Check this out.

"Riley says you've got twenty-four hours to write the check."

He looks at me with the eyes and fury of a boiled owl. When he speaks, his words are measured, precise, and seething with anger.

"You know what she is, Dani? A cunt."

What? What the fuck did he just call her?

I lean over, grab my handbag, start reaching inside for my gun. But before I get a good grip on it, he says, "Two million."

I stop what I'm doing and cock my head.

"Yeah, you heard me right. Tell the bitch I'll give her two million. But she's got to prove she's got the evidence to blackmail my son, and she's got to turn it over to me. And the payment is contingent on securing a maximum charge of voyeurism. Nothing more."

"She wants the money paid as a donation to her personal charity."

He frowns. "What charity?"

"She said she'd give me the details when you're ready to write the check. Apparently she's raising money to help underprivileged children get scholarships to private schools."

"Well, how fucking nice," he says, with a sneer. "What a saint! I wish she was *my* fucking client. That story ought to play pretty damn good in court."

"You think she's making it up?"

"I have no doubt she's registered a charity."

"I understand she's raised several thousand dollars so far."

"Well, la-de-fricken-da. I guess my two million dollar contribution will help her attract matching funds from schools all over the country. Before you know it the bitch will be paying herself a salary to run a hundred million dollar charity. She'll be set for life."

"I'll deliver the message."

"You do that."

I stand to leave. He says, "She'll take it, right?"

"I don't know."

"What do you mean? Why wouldn't she take it?"

I shrug. "I thought she'd take the first offer."

"The million?"

"Uh huh."

He says, "Because, who wouldn't, right? And now I've *doubled* it."

He's right. Of course she'll take it. Why? Because right now she's got nothing. And Gavin's right, her case sucks. The court won't let her sue for damages because the molesters are juveniles. She's suffered personal and public humiliation, and the boys who caused all the problems are going to wind up with no worse than a slap on the hand. We're talking two million dollars! Tax-free, since the money will be deposited in her charity. Of course she'll take it.

And yet...

I wouldn't mind making Gavin squirm a little more. So, from some dark, ugly place deep inside me, I allow myself to say, "If you want my honest opinion, I think she's going to say no."

"*What?* "*Why?*" He's practically pleading.

"I can't explain it, Gavin. She seems so sure of herself. Not cocky, exactly, just...totally confident. I'm not sure what you guys are talking about with regard to the birth certificates, but she didn't bat an eye over the million dollar offer. I've never met anyone quite like her at seventeen years of age."

"Fuck her," he says. "Fuck her to hell and back."

"I'll make the offer," I say.

I get as far as his office door.

"Three million," he says. "And not a penny more."

My legs nearly go out from under me. I try to contain my enthusiasm, but it's hard. I can't describe how proud I am that I gave in to my ugly streak. Because in the span of thirty seconds I just got Riley an extra million dollars!

"I'll tell her!"

"Dani?"

"Yes?"

"Make sure she knows that's my final offer. Anything more, and I'll take my chances in court."

"I'll tell her."

"Be firm."

"Count on it."

I start to leave again, and he says, "You'd take it, wouldn't you?"

Would I?

I think about it.

"Yes. Absolutely."

Of course, I'm not Riley Freeman.

Chapter 38

"If we keep meeting like this, my mom's going to think we're having sex," Riley says.

"Not funny," I say. "Sophie's already giving me shit about it."

"That aside," she says, "You look like the cat that swallowed the canary. What happened?"

"Like I said on the phone, I had a very interesting chat with Gavin."

"Tell me."

"He went to two million dollars on his own. But I told him I didn't think you'd take it."

She laughs. "Good girl! And he responded?"

"He went to three million! Riley, can you just imagine? Three million dollars! In cash!"

"Impressive. Thank you, Dani."

"I told him he'd have to donate the money to your charity, and said you'd give me the details."

"All true," she says. "Except for one thing."

"What's that?"

"This is going to cost him *six* million, not three."

"Slap my face!"

"What?"

"Punch my eye. Right here, where it's nearly swollen shut. That's the most painful area."

"What on earth are you *talking* about?"

"That way I'll know this isn't a dream."

She laughs. "It's not a dream, Dani. If Gavin wants this to go away, it's going to cost him six million."

"What's the extra million for?"

"Insulting me with this offer after I was nice enough to let him out for five. Why are you frowning?"

"Because I hate to be out of the loop."

"What do you mean?"

"What am I missing, Riley? What do you and Gavin know that I don't?"

She gives me a sly look. "Promise you won't tell?"

Chapter 39

"According to the live birth records Mona had in her possession, which I now have in mine, Ethan Clark was born twice."

"Fine," I say, pouting. "Don't tell me."

"I just did."

"Right. Thanks for nothing."

"Dani? I'm serious."

"So what are you saying? That Ethan's the world's first documented case of reincarnation?"

She laughs. "Indulge me."

"I thought I was."

"Story time. Allison Bennett came from the wealthiest, most prestigious family in Memphis, Tennessee. Gavin Clark knew he hit the mother lode when he knocked her up. Fearing the family name could never handle the scandal, they managed to pull together a legendary wedding in the space of ten weeks, which was really pressing it, since Allison was five months pregnant at the alter. After the wedding, she and Gavin went on a prolonged honeymoon, courtesy of Allison's parents. They were taking six months to travel the world. Over the next six months, family and friends received letters postmarked from the world's most exotic locations. In truth, Allison wrote all the letters beforehand, gave them to Mona, and Mona traveled to the destinations and sent the letters."

"That seems like a lot of trouble to go through. The Bennett family couldn't have been that concerned about people finding out their daughter had sex before marriage. This wasn't *that* long ago."

"High society, Dani. As they say, the rich are different than you and me."

"No kidding. So what happened?"

"Gavin and Allison were tucked away on the Bennett's private estate in California. The plan was to have a midwife deliver their baby at the estate. Four months later, Allison's father would secure a live birth certificate from a small hospital in Nevada, in return for a generous contribution. Instead of going back to Memphis, the young couple would begin their new life together here in Nashville, where Gavin's marital connections would quickly earn him a full partnership in a local law firm."

"So what went wrong?"

"Toward the end of Allison's pregnancy, she became violently ill, and nearly died from dehydration. They had to call an ambulance. She was rushed to the hospital, where, two weeks later, she gave birth to a little boy. She named him Ethan."

"Then what happened?"

"They stuck to the original plan. Four months later they got the phony birth certificate from Nevada, and they've been using that one ever since."

"How did they hide it from friends and family? The fact they were raising a four-month-old instead of a newborn?"

"They were in a different city, remember? And they kept a low profile that first year. After that, no one questioned their kid looking a few months older than the others his age."

"Mona told you all this?"

"She did."

"So let's see if I understand. Ethan has two birth certificates, four months apart, from two different states."

"That's right. And both show a live birth delivered to the same parents."

"Which is impossible."

"Exactly."

"And Ethan and his parents used the newer one, which is phony, because it kept Memphis society from finding out Allison got knocked up before the wedding."

"That's correct."

"I'm going to go out on a limb and guess that the older birth certificate, the real one, shows that Ethan is eighteen years old. And was, when he molested you last week."

"To be precise," Riley says, "he was eighteen years and nine days old on that fateful night."

"Which means he can be tried as an adult."

"By Jove, I think you've got it," she says.

"Which means if your attorney pushes for sexual assault, he could do prison time."

"That's stretching it. I mean, we're still talking about a stupidly rich family, with lots of connections. But it does mean his name could be spread all over the country, and I'd be able to sue him in civil court."

"What type of award could you get in a civil lawsuit?"

"Now that the photos have hit the internet? Two or three million, easily."

"Which Gavin has already offered you. Without the hassle of a lawsuit"

"True, but what's the Clark and Bennett family name worth?"

"What do you mean?"

"If the court finds out Ethan's eighteen, even if he escapes jail time, he'll be a registered sex offender.

"Holy shit!" I say.

"Exactly."

"So the number's six million?"

"It is. And Dani, I know it sounds like I'm taking advantage of the situation, but I guarantee he'd pay twice that much. This is a drop in the bucket for a guy who contributes three million a year to crooked politicians. I'm not exaggerating, I looked it up. And don't forget, unlike his donations to politicians, he'll get a tax deduction for this. Yes, this whole thing is nasty business. But I didn't ask for it. And so far I'm the only one who's had to suffer public humiliation for it. Gavin can keep it that way and help something good come out of all this by making a one-time contribution to a charity that will help me change people's lives."

"You make a helluva case," I say.

211

The front door of her house opens. A woman comes out and stands on the porch and stares at my car.

"Your mom?" I say.

"She's not too subtle, is she?"

"Let me guess. She's heard I'm gay?"

"Once the toothpaste is out of the tube, there's no pushing it back in."

"Well, I don't blame her for being nervous," I say. "I'm six years older, the windows are fogged, and I keep showing up to meet you in the car. Probably looks bad from her point of view."

We look at her mom a minute. Then Riley says, "I'll be a good steward of that money, Dani."

"I believe you."

She adds, "Deserving kids are going to benefit from this. And if that means crooked politicians have to live without bribes for the next two years, I'd call it a good trade."

"I agree. I'll give him the message."

She pauses. Then says, "Based on what you know of him, and what I've said about Ethan's age, what's your opinion? You think he'll write the check?"

I sigh. "Honestly? I think you're reaching. The time element already made this a tough sale. Now you're rubbing his nose in it by adding an extra million."

"You think I'm gouging him."

"This is your party, Riley. I'm just delivering the cake."

"What would you do if you were me?"

"I would've taken the million. So you *know* I'd take the three."

We're quiet a minute, two women sitting in a car, in the dark, under the watchful gaze of a concerned mother.

When her mom starts flipping the porch light on and off, Riley says, "I agree."

That surprises me.

"You'll take the three million?" I say.

"No. The number's still six. But I agree he's going to say no."

The porch lights flicker faster, almost like a strobe light.

I say, "But you still want me to tell him six million?"

"Yes."

"And if he says no?"

"Then hand him this."

She unzips a pocket on the right thigh of her cargo pants and removes a CD, places it in my hand.

"Riley! Omigod! Is this—"

"Don't ask. But promise me something."

"What?"

"Do *not* show this to Gavin unless you're convinced he won't pay the six million."

"You want me to play it for him or give it to him?"

"Give it to him, and tell him it's a copy. But promise you won't watch it."

"You can't be serious!"

"Please, Dani. You have to promise me."

"That's bullshit, Riley. I need to see what happened. I've put a lot of time into this case. You said it yourself, I'm emotionally invested. You have to let me see it. Otherwise, it'll eat at me the rest of my life."

"Dani, I'm counting on you not to watch it. I really want to believe in you. Everything I will ever think about

213

you from this point forward hangs on your promise. If it's too much to ask, tell me now, and I'll have it couriered to Gavin tonight."

I sigh. "Seriously, Riley?"

"Please, Dani."

I sigh again, shake my head. "Fine. You have my solemn promise."

"Thanks, Dani."

She hands me two slips of paper.

"What's this?"

"One is the information about my charity."

"And the other?"

"A check made out to you from my charity. Post-dated."

"That is so sweet of you," I say. "But I can't accept it. That would make me a party to the transaction."

"You *are* party to the transaction. You're the go-between."

"Yes. And if anyone ever shows up to ask me what part I played, I'd like to be able to claim neutrality."

"So you won't let me pay you anything for all your work?"

"Do you have a dollar on you?"

She reaches in her pocket. "I have three ones and two fives."

"I'll accept one dollar, as your paid messenger, to deliver this CD to Gavin Clark, without personally watching it. How's that?"

"Deal!" she says. "Thanks, Dani!"

She hands me the dollar, and kisses my cheek.

The passenger door suddenly flies open, startling us.

Riley's mom shouts, "I *knew* it! Get the *fuck* off my property, whore, and leave my daughter alone!"

Riley scrambles out of the car and shouts, "Thanks for the sex, Dani!" Then laughs when her mom shouts, "You think that's funny?"

I shake my head. It's tough being me. I start the car and put it in drive. Then call Gavin, who answers with, "What did she say? Did she agree to the three million?"

"I haven't had time to talk to her yet."

"Why not?"

"Her mom interrupted us. But it's okay. Riley will be back out any second. I just wanted you to know I'll be a few minutes late."

"I'll be here when you get here."

I hang up, then drive to my office, fire up my computer, remove the CD from its case, and slide it in my CD drive.

Chapter 40

I'm keeping my promise to Riley. I agreed not to watch the CD, and I won't. But I didn't agree not to make a copy.

Am I splitting hairs?

Of course. Look, I'm sorry, but I did *not* go through all this just to walk away while the answer is literally in my hands.

I have to see what happened.

I have to know. And don't get all high and mighty with me, because you would have done the exact same thing.

So don't even go there!

After making the copy, I put it in my safe, unwatched. Then I put the original CD in my handbag, and drive to Gavin's office.

"What did she say?" he says, before I even manage to take a seat. Then he says, "I should have stuck to the two million, shouldn't I? The minute you left I regretted going to three. No way she would've turned down two million."

"But you *did* say three, right?" I say, ugly streak still intact.

His face falls. "Fuck. Two million would have done it. I *knew* it!"

"Don't beat yourself up about it," I say. "She turned you down."

"Sh-she *what*? *What*? She turned—*what*?"

He's really upset. This is no longer fun for me. I don't enjoy seeing anyone squirm like this.

He yells, "You told her three million, right? What are you talking about, she turned me down?"

I don't hate him as much as I did when I thought he erased the photos on the boys' phones. That would have made him guilty of destroying evidence. What he's really guilty of is loving a rotten son, and cleaning up after him his whole life instead of letting Ethan take responsibility for his actions. Yes, Gavin's shady. And I'm not sure what role he might've played in Parker Page's confession. Or why he got it from her in the first place. Or how he planned to use it. But like I said, I'm not enjoying this.

I'm not looking forward to telling him about the extra million she's demanding, either.

He yells, "I'm not sure you're representing me properly, Ms. Ripper! I think you might be working against me! What the fuck is going on here? If I find out you're milking this situation, I'll—"

But here's the thing: I don't *hate* mentioning it, either. It's kind of nice to see the bully get a beating.

"She said no to your three million, but she made you a counter."

I hand him the piece of paper with the information about her charity.

"What's her number?" he says. "Three-point-five?"

"Six."

"Three-point-six?"

"No, sir. Six million."

"Get the fuck out of here!"

"Seriously? You want me to leave?"

"No, asshole. It's an expression. What the hell are you talking about? What happened to five million?"

"She said your counter was an insult. She feels the case is worth twelve million. She thinks you're getting off easy."

"This fucking gutter snipe thinks I'm getting off too easy by blackmailing me to the tune of six million dollars?"

"I don't think she considers it blackmail."

"Explain the logic behind that comment."

"You offered her a million dollars to go along with a lesser charge. She countered your offer."

"By threatening to expose something that could cause a royal shit storm! I don't know what constitutes blackmail in Cincinnati, where you're from," he says. "But here in Nashville, a rectum's the same as an asshole."

"Do you plan to charge her with blackmail?"

"For six million dollars I will."

"Can I make a recommendation?"

"What?"

"Pay the money."

"*What?*"

"You should pay it and move on."

"Out of the question! Preposterous!"

"Why?"

"By raising the offer, she's already proven she can't be trusted. Dollars to donuts that little whore will find a way to leak the evidence. She's probably in cahoots with Parker. Probably got Parker to put the photos on the internet in the first place. What's going to keep her from putting this other shit on the internet?"

"I understand you're upset. But I can't abide you calling Riley a whore. And while we're at it, don't you *ever* use the "C" word in my presence again, as long as you live. You must know how offensive it is."

"For six million dollars I'll say any fucking words I want."

His comment puts me in mind of Jana Bagger, may she rest in peace.

"Don't think of it as blackmail," I say. "Think of it as a tax deduction. You're going to come out of this looking like a hero. Your son pleads guilty to a momentary lapse of judgment, but you feel so badly for Riley you contribute six million dollars to her charity, to help underprivileged kids get scholarships to private schools. You'll get incredible press for it, and Ethan won't suffer any permanent damage to his reputation."

"No. I will not be shaken down by this two-bit whore."

"I'm warning you, Gavin. For the last time."

He glares at me, then says, "Fine. I'll try to watch my language. But my answer is no."

"Sleep on it."

"No. I'm drawing the line."

"This is your pride talking. Think of all the ramifications."

"Ethan will just have to roll the dice. It's time he took responsibility for his actions. You can tell little Miss Strawberry

219

Snatch that the legal system is often what the attorneys and judges say it is. Tell her other people can leak shit, too. Like maybe her best friend's confession got taped, and *that* shows up on the internet. What does *that* do to Riley's precious case? And don't forget, there is no conclusive evidence of sexual assault. Try to shake *me* down for six million dollars? Well, fuck *her!*"

"Is that a no?"

His face looks meaner than a carbuncle.

"It's a no. Tell her I'm going to bury her. I'll make it my life's mission."

"Is that your final answer?"

"Final and forever. And damn her to hell!"

I stand, start walking to the door.

He says, "Wait."

I turn.

"If I offer her the original five million, what do you think she'll say?"

"I think she'll say seven. Or eight."

He sighs. "I think so too."

I wait.

He says, "What if I demand to be on her charity's board of directors?"

"She'll say no."

He nods.

I wait some more.

His face appears to age ten years before the words come out.

"I'll pay the six million," he says.

I'd tell you how shocked I am, but I'm not even mildly surprised. That's why I stood up and walked to the door without handing him the CD. I knew he'd stop me before I walked out the door. Knew he'd pay Riley's price.

I look at him, wrung out, slumped in his chair, hair all over the place, head in his hands. This is what a thoroughly beaten man looks like.

It's not a pretty sight.

I say, "Can I ask you a question?"

"What?"

"How does one go about dotting the "I's" and crossing the "T's" on this type of deal?"

His voice comes out in a low monotone, as if adding inflection might cost him extra. He says, "Everyone's forced to trust each other. Nothing will be in writing, but we'll both have to show good faith. I'll give her a certified check on Monday and she'll give me the evidence she's using to blackmail me. She'll tell me she's given me everything, but we'll both know she's lying. But that won't stop her from fulfilling her end of the bargain. If she does, everyone wins. If she fudges on the deal, I'll find a way to destroy her through her charity. There are a hundred ways I can rig a scandal, and she knows it. The likelihood is, everything will work out, and we'll publicly pretend we're friends. You're right, I'll probably look like a warm-hearted hero for a while. Even as she's dissecting my nut sack."

"Will you be in touch with her from this point on?"

"No. She'll have an attorney. No one will know about this. You've already signed a confidential agreement, and I can't stress enough how badly things will go for you if you tell anyone what happened here. I'll give you the certified check on Monday. You'll take it to Riley, and she'll hold it until the sentencing phase takes place. After that, she'll deposit it, and probably schedule a press release. Tell her I'm open to that, but I want to see her draft and have the right to make changes."

"Okay."

I say goodbye, reassure him he's made the right decision, head out the door, and walk to my car. I climb in, turn on the engine, lower the seat till I'm comfortable, and lie there, listening to the radio.

Thirty minutes pass, then forty.

Then he calls.

"Where are you?"

"In my car, in your parking lot."

"Why?"

"I've been waiting for you to call, to tell me you've changed your mind."

"You're right. I have. It's just not worth six million."

"Yes it is, Gavin."

"No, it's not. I've looked at it from every angle. I'm willing to take my chances in court."

"In that case, I have one last thing to give you."

"I'm coming down."

When I hand him the CD he says, "What's this supposed to be?"

"I can't say for certain, because I haven't seen it. But I'm pretty sure it's a video of everything that happened to Riley Saturday night."

He has to put his hand on the roof of my car to keep from falling down. I expect him to yell and scream, or cry, or possibly drop to the ground and curl up in a fetal position, but he does none of those things.

Instead, his face breaks into a wide grin.

"Why didn't you give me this earlier?" he says.

"She made me promise only to give it to you as a last resort."

"I could kiss you right now!" he shouts.

"I've got a gun that says you can't."

I show him my gun, just to make sure.

"She went too far," he chortles.

"What do you mean?"

"She bet the house and lost. If this is, in fact, video evidence of the event in question, it proves the whole thing was a setup. You don't have to let me kiss you, but I certainly owe you dinner. Because you didn't just save me six million dollars, young lady. You saved my son's reputation. And the agony of a legal battle."

I sigh.

"What's wrong?"

"This has been a bad day for you," I say. "And it's about to get worse."

"Why's that?"

"Riley didn't make this video."

"Of course she did."

"No. Mitch Underhill made it."

"Who?"

"Kelli's stepfather. Mitch installed cameras in Kelli's bedroom last year. He's been taping her ever since. His wife, Lydia, found dozens of CDs yesterday. They believe it's the reason he committed suicide today."

223

"He was spying on his own daughter?"

"Stepdaughter. And his surveillance equipment was running when Riley passed out in Kelli's room."

Though the parking lot is dimly lit, I can see Gavin aging again, right before my eyes. Like one of those time-lapse videos that takes less than a minute to see a guy losing weight over the course of a year.

"Have the police seen this?"

"I only have personal knowledge of two copies existing in the world. And this is one of them."

"Have you seen it?"

"I have not. Riley made me swear a solemn oath not to look at it. Even with you."

"It must be really bad."

"I can't imagine her giving it to you if it wasn't."

"I'll watch it tonight, and let you know tomorrow."

"Okay."

He turns and walks back toward the front of his office building, each step slower than the preceding one. As if he doesn't really want to reach his destination. In fact, he's walking so slowly I fear he might die of old age before he gets to the door.

I put my car in gear and head back to my office.

When I get there, I find the place ransacked. The door of my safe has been pried open. There's nothing inside.

It takes a moment before I realize I'm never going to know what was on that tape.

I'll never know the truth of what happened to Riley at the slumber party.

And neither will you.

Chapter 41

I'm lying.

No one's been in my office, no one broke into my safe, no one stole my CD.

I was just messing with you.

I open the safe, remove the CD, take it to my computer, and pop it in the slot.

Chapter 42

The tape has been edited to show only the Riley clip. In other words, whatever happened before and after is not shown.

But the tape shows everything that happened to Riley.

In graphic detail.

Since you're not likely to ever see it, I'll go through it for you, step-by-step, in Chapter 43. I won't give vivid explanations of the most extreme parts, but I won't omit them, either. I'll explain what's happening in a clinical, non-erotic way, wherever possible. But in the event you have no interest in hearing what's on the tape, please skip Chapter 43 and go directly to Chapter 44.

Chapter 43

Riley told the truth.

There are two camera angles, merged into a split-screen. The left side shows the view from the dresser, ten feet from the foot of Kelli's bed. The right side shows an overhead view. If you want to see what happened in general, without the graphic detail, you can cover the right side of the screen.

The cameras begin rolling when the light comes on, and what you see at the beginning is a young girl in pajamas, clearly Riley Freeman, entering the room. She stops a moment to sit on the corner of the bed. She's holding her stomach. There is sound, but she's silent, except for an occasional heavy sigh, as if she's in mild discomfort. She leans her head down, hair covering her face, then puts her head in her hands.

From the left camera you can see the bathroom door is open. Riley gets up on shaky legs, and makes her way to the bathroom, where she puts a hand against the wall to steady

227

herself before entering. She goes in, and closes the bathroom door behind her.

Since the lights are still on, the cameras continue to run. Minutes go by, without a sound. There is no sound of a toilet flushing, but I hear water running for a few seconds. Then it stops, and the door opens. As Riley comes out I notice a hand towel in her left hand that falls to the floor behind her. She staggers to the bed and sits there a minute, staring blankly. Then she slowly eases herself onto her right side, facing the bedroom door, and lies there fifteen seconds before scooting to the middle of the bed.

When Riley gave me her explanation of these events, limited as it was, for some reason I envisioned her lying on her back the entire time. But that's not what happened. She's on her side, knees close to her stomach. Both cameras show her pajama shirt riding up slightly in the back, revealing approximately three inches of her lower back.

She has not positioned herself in a sexy manner. In other words, if this had been staged, I would expect the presentation to be far more erotic.

Within minutes, she's clearly unconscious.

Ethan Lied.

By my count, six minutes pass before the door is opened. I'm expecting the light to go off and the camera to shut down, which would indicate Parker Page has entered the room to check on Riley. I study the video very carefully to see the break in the tape that shows the camera went off and then back on.

To my surprise, the cameras continue to roll. There is no break or gap in the video because the light is never turned off. As further evidence the cameras have not stopped, I hear someone speaking just before the door opens. The voice is male, and melodic in a creepy sing-song way, as if he's playing hide-and-seek. He says, "*Ri*-ley, oh *Ri*-ley! Where *are* you, Riley? Are you in here?"

Two teenage boys, our own Ethan Clark and Ronnie English—enter the room. Ethan's doing the talking.

"*Ri*-ley," he says, clearly inebriated. He notices her on the bed and says, "Well, what do we have here?"

"Holy shit!" Ronnie says. "Dude!"

"*Ri*-ley," Ethan sings.

He slaps her ass.

"Damn!" he says. "She didn't even move!"

"No way!" Ronnie says.

"Dude! Shut the door!"

Ronnie does. Then, in a voice quivering with excitement, says, "Oh, my God! This is great. Wait. She's probably faking."

"I don't think so, man. Check this out."

The overhead camera shows Ethan shaking her shoulder. He says, "Dude, this is one fucked-up bitch!"

"No way!"

"You know what this is?" Ethan says. "A gift from God."

"Like sacrificing a virgin," Ronnie says. "Except backwards."

Ethan looks at his friend and says, "Dude. You're killing the mood with that shit. That is just weird."

"What if we're being set up?"

"It'll be *worth* it!"

"Man, I don't trust anyone. Look under the bed."

"*You* look under the bed, asshole."

"Fine. But you should check the closet, just to be sure."

"I'll check the bathroom, *you* check the closet."

Ronnie looks under the bed, then checks the closet. The left camera shows Ethan disappear into the bathroom a few seconds. Then he comes out and sits on the bed to Riley's right, facing her back.

"You know how many times I've checked out your ass, Miss Riley?" Ethan says.

"A million times?" Ronnie offers.

"A million and six."

"But you never saw it."

"No one has, I don't think."

"She's probably faking," Ronnie says.

"I can find out."

"Do it."

Ethan pauses. "Promise you won't tell?"

"Who the fuck would I tell?"

"Ri-ley," Ethan sings, "Last chance, baby doll. If you're faking, tell me now, 'cause I'm gonna pull your pants down."

"Do it!" Ronnie says. "I dare you!"

Ethan hesitates. Says, "I'll leave it up to Riley." He whispers, "Riley?" Then says, in a louder voice, "If it's okay, don't say a word. If you're okay with me pulling your pants down, keep quiet. If you *don't* want me to touch you, just say so."

Ronnie raises his voice an octave, imitating a girl. "Pull my pants down, Ethan!"

"If you insist," he says.

Ronnie moves across the room to Ethan's side. "Do it!" he whispers.

"Check it out!" Ethan whispers back, as he slides her pants and panties down.

"Oh, my God!" Ronnie says. "I'm gonna blow a load right here!"

"*Dude!*" Ethan whispers. "Act like you've been here before. What's your problem?"

He says, "Go outside and guard the door."

"No way!"

"Dude! Guard the fuckin' door! We'll take turns."

"How long till my turn?"

"Five minutes."

"Bullshit! One minute."

"Two."

Ronnie says, "All right. Two. Then it's my turn."

Ethan says, "Don't rush the count."

Ronnie moves swiftly to the door, saying, "Want me to turn the lights off?"

"No way, man. I want to see what she's been keeping from me all these years."

After further consideration...

I've decided to sum up. Some things are better left unsaid. Here's the short version: over the next two-and-a-half minutes, Ethan pulls up Riley's shirt, pulls her pants and panties down to her ankles, touches her, fondles her, performs oral.

Then something happens.

Riley starts to move.

Ethan jumps back.

Riley murmurs, "What are you doing?"

Ethan whispers, "Shhh. Nothing. Go back to sleep."

He pauses while she seems to drift unconscious again. He uses his mouth again and she murmurs. "Don't. Please. Please...stop."

Her words are hard to make out, because they seem to come from a far-away place. And yet, they're clear enough to me, watching the video, which means Ethan had no problem hearing and understanding her.

But he doesn't stop. He says, "What did you say, baby? You *like* it? Huh? You *like* it? Well, I like it *too*! I like it a lot!"

Riley murmurs something I can't make out. Ethan says, "Oh, I'll stop. Yeah, that's right, baby, I'll stop. When I'm good and ready!"

The door opens. Ronnie comes in and says, "Holy shit, Dude! That's enough! My turn."

Ethan looks up and says, "Can't do it, man."

"What?"

"I can't let you do it."

"What do you mean?"

"I'll let you see her. That's only fair. But I can't let you touch her."

"But—"

"Sorry, dude. Not gonna happen. It's not cool."

"What the fuck are you *talkin'* about?"

"Close the door and come here. I'll give you a quick look."

Ronnie closes the door, rushes back. "I'm taking pictures."

"Good idea."

Ethan says, "Want to see her snatch? Of course you do. Show him your snatch, Riley. Yeah, that's right. Photo op!"

They take several shots from different angles.

Ethan says, "Check it out, Ron."

"Bingo!"

They take another shot.

"Boobs?" Ethan says. "Nice, right? Photo op!"

He rolls her over.

"It's all nice, my man. From top to bottom. Wait. One more. Don't be modest, Riley, you're among friends. Photo op!"

He pauses a second, then says, "Okay, you're done, Ronald. Guard the door, I'll get her dressed."

He does. Then takes a photo of her fully dressed, on her back. This is the photo Rick Hooper sent. I never would have believed Gavin's claim that Ethan dressed her first, then took the picture, could possibly be true. Of course, Gavin never would have believed everything else his son did.

Do I feel sorry for Gavin?

I do, a little.

No parent should have to see his son committing a sex crime.

A minute goes by, then the tape cuts off.

Bottom line?

One, Parker was not involved. Two, Ethan committed sexual assault. Forcibly, since Riley clearly asked him to stop. Three, he also committed forcible oral sexual intercourse. Four, Ronnie is guilty of voyeurism.

It's clear why Riley didn't want me to see the video. She knows I'd throw a fit, turn it over to the police, and demand jail time for Ethan. Of course, I can't do that, having signed a non-disclosure and confidentiality agreement that covers anything and everything I heard, saw, handled, and learned through my conversations with Riley and Gavin.

I feel sick for Riley.

On the other hand, I know the stats. The majority of rapes in America go unreported. Convictions are hard to secure. And convicted rapists often spend less than four years in prison.

Riley made the choice that works for her. Her charity will receive six million dollars, and I have no doubt she'll put the money to good use. I also have no doubt she'll fulfill the terms of her settlement with Gavin, and take the extra step of making sure he gets warm and fuzzy press coverage for his massive contribution.

Chapter 44

Monday.

We're sitting in a coffee shop, not far from Riley's house, when I hand her the check.

She glances at it, then studies my face.

"Aw, shit, Dani."

"What's wrong?"

"You watched the video."

"I—Yes. I made a copy. I watched it, then destroyed it."

"You broke your promise."

"Yes."

"You may have also broken a law, since you knowingly viewed underage sex."

"Don't be ridiculous. I had no prior knowledge there'd be sexual activity on that CD. Plus, this was my case, and you're my friend and client."

"Client?"

"My one-dollar client."

"Ah!" she says.

Her face clouds up. "I'm sorry you saw that. It was pretty brutal stuff. That had to be hard on you."

"It was. But it would've been much worse had it been real."

"What do you mean?"

"I thought about it all weekend. And realized you set him up."

She looks at me oddly. Then, in a very polite, conversational tone, asks, "Why would you say that?"

"It's all too pat."

"What is?"

"Everything."

"Name one."

"The timing window."

"What's that?"

"You had to wait till Kelli's mom went to bed. You also had to count on her being unable to hear any possible activity, such as two semi-drunk teenage boys going up and down the steps and in and out of Kelli's bedroom. So you couldn't count on precise timing for that. Then, once the mom is down for the night, you have to coordinate getting the boys there, getting you into Kelli's room, getting the boys into the house, into the basement, singling Ethan out, getting him, and as it turns out, Ronnie, up the stairs in time to find you passed out, on Kelli's bed, and all this has to happen before Parker's mom picks her up, or else Parker won't be there to run interference on the rest of the gang in the basement."

"You don't feel those few events could occur naturally?"

"No."

"Maybe that's because you're looking at it as a conspiracy," Riley says. "The timing issues only seem difficult because you're trying to make them fit your theory."

"Got a better one?"

"Yes, but it's awfully simple."

"Tell me."

"If Mrs. Underhill didn't happen to go to bed early, Kelli wouldn't have let the boys come over. And none of this would have happened."

"But it did happen. And Parker was the key to all the timing issues. She got Ethan where he needed to be. Ronnie followed. She got them all worked up, told them about the sticker, dared them to find and photograph it."

She laughs. "You must have watched a different video. I don't recall seeing Parker at all on the one I watched."

"Here's the thing: you're incredibly good. The whole Parker confession threw me off. But the more I thought about it, the more I decided the first part of Ethan's story was true. I think she coordinated everything, right down to challenging them to find the sticker."

"I don't recall them saying anything about finding the sticker on the video."

"Me either, and I think you got lucky with that, though no doubt, they were distracted. But remember near the end? When Ethan let Ronnie take pictures?"

"What about it?"

"There was a point when Ethan said, 'Check it out, Ron,' and Ronnie responded, 'Bingo!'"

"So?"

"I couldn't figure out why Ronnie would say 'Bingo!' Then it dawned on me he was talking about the sticker. The one he'd been told about."

"That's quite a stretch."

"I agree, which is why I think you were lucky he didn't come right out and say something like, 'Parker was right! There it is!'"

She smiles. "That's your Ronnie impression?"

I smile back. Then say, "Parker got them all worked up, then went back to the party and told the others Ethan and Ronnie were outside, going through their cars for liquor."

"What motive would she have for doing all that?"

"The ten thousand Gavin paid for her so-called confession?"

"How on earth could she have known that would happen?"

"She couldn't. But it's all I've got."

"Everything doesn't have to fit into a neat little theory, Dani."

I think a moment. "You didn't happen to offer Parker a job, did you? Working for your foundation? Assuming your plan worked and you were able to secure funding?"

Riley smiles. "Parker's extremely intelligent, and a hard worker. I would *love* to have her helping me. But she has plans for college."

"Kelli also had to be involved."

"How so?"

"I think she found out about the cameras on her own some time ago, and told you Mitch had been secretly filming her. I think she wanted revenge, and you both planned it out. You picked Ethan because his father understood the law and because you had killer information regarding his birth certificate. And that's another timing issue that bothered me. You kept that birth certificate information quiet until the negotiating phase. And while we're on the subject, let's not forget the on-again, off-again video you saved till the last possible second. Your closing argument, if you will."

"You make me sound like a mastermind."

"You are. And I'm in awe."

She takes a "let's wrap this up" tone, saying, "Dani, I can always count on you for entertaining conversation. We should do this again sometime, after the legal system works out all the details."

"The photographs Dillon took."

"What about them?"

"In the wee hours of Sunday morning I'm watching the video on the same computer that had the photos Dillon took of Kelli's room. And it dawned on me how you made a point to get my attention focused on the first four photos, the ones he took with the flash. I didn't get it at the time, but you were trying to get me to see the reflection of the camera lenses. You must have been disappointed in me that day. Of course, Fanny came through, so you didn't have to come up with something more obvious."

Riley shrugs.

I say, "And what about the CDs in Mitch's room?"

"What about them?"

"There's been no mention of CDs, videos, or video surveillance equipment being found in Mitch's room. Police were there, investigating his death. Even the news reporters have nothing to say about the presence of video equipment."

"So?"

"Doesn't that strike you as odd?"

"I guess I've been so busy with my own issues, I haven't taken time to think about that."

"I have."

"What do you think happened?"

"I think you, Parker, and Kelli removed all the equipment from Mitch's room after making your video. I think you destroyed all the evidence except your video. I think you went through Mitch's room with a fine-tooth comb last week, and probably caught a break since his and Kelli's rooms were on the second floor."

"How does that help?"

"The wiring between the two rooms went through the attic, and was easy to find. Then, sometime after Dillon took pictures of Kelli's bedroom, and you knew we finally figured out there were cameras, you removed them from Kelli's room. Then, when Mitch came home, I think Kelli confronted him and told him she watched all the videos, called the police, and they showed up and confiscated everything. I can practically hear her saying, 'They're gathering evidence even as we speak. They're going to see video evidence that you raped me. And by the way, the police have already issued a warrant for your arrest. They're coming to get you, Mitch!' I think he was devastated that all this was about to come out. I think Kelli may have talked Mitch into committing suicide. If she didn't kill him herself."

She looks around the coffee shop, then gives me a sympathetic smile and says, "Please tell me you're not wearing a wire, hoping to bait me into confessing something that might give credibility to this outlandish tale."

"I'm not wearing a wire. We can go in the restroom right now and I'll prove it, if you'll tell me how you managed to put all this together."

She studies the check carefully. Then says, "This is what you thought about all weekend?"

"It is."

"And when did you come to the crazy conclusion the whole thing was a setup?"

"Last night."

"And yet you still went to Gavin today and collected the check?"

"I did."

"Why?"

"Because I'm on your side, Riley. I always have been, and probably always will be. Don't get me wrong, I don't like what you did. But I'm okay with it."

"Let's pretend for a minute your accusations are true. How could you possibly be okay with it?"

"I make my living doing decoy work."

"So?"

"People pay me to test other people's characters. It's usually wives or fiancés paying to see if their husbands or future husbands can be trusted. I find the mark, tease him, tantalize him. Make him prove his character. At the point I can prove he's faithful, or not, I turn the evidence over to the person who hired me."

"You must have had some close calls."

"Good point. Which is why I always have an ally close by, someone who can protect me in case things go too far. When I'm on a date with a mark I do my best to keep him from getting drunk, but as you well know, it's not an exact science. You get a guy all worked up, he might go too far."

"Interesting."

"I'm always concerned at the end of the evening when the moment of truth arrives, because it usually involves a hotel room, or a car, or even an elevator. My biggest fear is he'll pull a knife on me, lock the elevator between two floors, and rape me."

"And you're telling me all this because?"

"I've had years of experience as a decoy. And even *I* wouldn't dare be alone in a room with two teenage boys who'd been drinking."

"You're asking me if I had an ally."

"I am."

"Why is this so important to you?"

"Because I've decided to focus on what I do best."

"Which is?"

"Decoy work."

"It does sound fascinating."

"Here's what I think. You may be young, but you're the best I've ever seen. You're a natural. Parker and Kelli might prove to be equally good as decoys, though they're obviously not mastermind material."

"Are you offering the three of us a job?"

"Yes. I want you to work with me. At least from time to time."

"Why would we possibly want to do that? I've got my charity, the girls have senior year and college coming up."

"You'd all have to be eighteen, of course. But as for why you might want to? Simple. It's exhilarating! The three of you put together the most intricate, innovative scam I've ever seen. And you're just getting started. You can't tell me you didn't feel an incredible rush, making all this happen. I've been there. It's euphoric. Intoxicating. Addictive. Good as you are? You're going to want more. Even when money isn't important to you anymore, you're going to miss the rush. You'll crave the excitement."

"You sound almost jealous not to be included."

"But I *was* included. I figured it out before getting the check today. I could have brought up all these concerns to Gavin."

"Could you have proven them?"

"As it turns out, yes."

Her expression turns serious.

"What are you talking about?"

"Everything I've mentioned raised a red flag. The timing, the CDs, the way you tried to get us focused on the photos, your prior knowledge of Ethan's birth certificate...but you're right, there was nothing I could prove."

"And yet?"

"Dumb luck reared its head..."

She waits.

"...In the form of panties."

243

"I have no idea what you're talking about," Riley says. "And that's the truth."

"I have a client who thought his wife, Erica, was cheating on him. Saturday, he brought me a pair of Erica's soiled, stained panties so I could test the semen residue."

"Dani. About that job offer? It's a no. A *firm* no."

"That's not part of the decoy job, it's from the business I'm trying to get away from. But hear me out. Yesterday I tracked Erica down and had a talk with her. And learned who she'd been sleeping with."

"Someone I know?"

"Mitch Underhill."

"That's an amazing coincidence. But where are you going with all this?"

"Can you imagine how shocked she must have been to hear he committed suicide only hours after they had sex?"

"That must have been very hard on her. Did her mood improve when you returned her panties?"

I smile.

She smiles.

"See? This is why I like you so much," I say. "Who else talks like this?"

"Thanks. As you talked with Erica, I suppose she confided in you about Mitch and his activities?"

"She told me what she knew, which wasn't much. Nothing for you to worry about. She said three months ago Mitch claimed to enjoy taping himself having sex with other women. He even admitted he was seeing someone else and wondered if Erica would consider a threesome."

"Did she?"

"No, but she pretended to be interested, so she could find out who the other woman was."

"Clever."

"So Mitch got all excited, and gave Erica a CD showing him having sex with the other woman. She asked if she could keep the CD because it really turned her on. Erica never confronted the other woman, but she did send her the CD."

"So Erica kept seeing Mitch even though he'd been dating another woman?"

"I know. Crazy, right?"

She shrugs.

I say, "Guess who the other woman was?"

"How would I know?"

"Please. Say it."

She looks around again. Then stands, and says, "I need to use the restroom. Want to freshen up?"

"I do."

We enter the restroom and wait till the lady who's in there finishes washing her hands. Then I place a small wedge into the door jamb, turn toward Riley, and raise my blouse to my neck. I turn in a circle. Then lower my blouse, raise my skirt to my waist, and make a circle. Then she looks through my handbag.

"You're *armed?*" she says.

"It's not as exciting as it sounds," I say. "I nearly shot Fanny by mistake on Friday."

She laughs. "Jesus, Dani."

"I know."

When she's satisfied I'm not wearing a wire, she says, "You wanted me to guess who Mitch filmed himself having sex with?"

"Uh huh."

"Parker Page."

"Bingo!"

She laughs. "Funny."

"One thing I've got to know," I say.

"What's that?"

"You're too smart to take a chance on having two teenage boys in that room with you. They'd been drinking. You must have had a backup. But I can't figure out who it was."

"Think about it."

"I have. There were eight boys in the basement, plus Kelli, and the two other girls she invited to the slumber party, Jennie Cox and Cammi Churra. And Parker, who had to be picked up by midnight. So who's left to mind the store?"

"Think about it."

"There's no one left."

"Think about it, Dani. What's the centerpiece of your timing issues?"

"That so much had to happen in such a small window of time."

"And who was central to that?"

"Parker."

She shakes her head. "Before Parker."

"Kelli."

"Jesus, Dani. Before Kelli."

I'm ashamed it takes me so long. But when it hits, it hits hard.

"I don't believe it!" I say.

She smiles. "*I'm* certainly not going to say it!"

I say, "Kelli's mom. Lydia Underhill! Can I get a Bingo?"

"Not from me," she says, laughing.

"How the hell?"

"That's all I'm going to say."

"You haven't said *anything*! How could she be your ally? How could she have possibly known if you'd need help when they were alone in the room with you?"

"Think about it."

"Not this again!"

"Where's the one place Lydia could have been that would allow her to protect me, if neccesary?"

"Holy shit! Mitch's bedroom! She watched the whole thing live. She coordinated with Parker, and Kelli, and she did it because she also hated Mitch."

I shake my head. "That was brilliant of you guys to have her attorney threaten me at the beginning of my investigation. It threw me off completely."

I think about it some more and say, "Wait. Did she kill Mitch?"

Riley says nothing.

I say, "She'd get next to nothing in a divorce. Same thing if he wound up in prison. But if he *died...*"

My mind races to the natural conclusions. "This all happened three months ago. Parker received the video from Erica, watched it and realized Mitch had filmed them having sex in Kelli's room. Parker knew the only way that could have happened is if Mitch had been filming his stepdaughter, Kelli.

"Parker must have freaked out. She'd been sleeping with Kelli's stepfather, who'd been filming Kelli. She told you about it, and the two of you broke the news to Kelli, who wondered if Mitch filmed himself raping her last year. She broke into Mitch's room not last week, but three months ago! Found the videos. Watched them, including her own rape. She couldn't keep the secret any longer, so she told her mom, and showed her the video.

"Kelli, Parker, and Lydia all wanted Mitch put away, but Kelli and Lydia didn't want to lose the lifestyle, and Kelli and Parker didn't want the police and everyone else in the world to see videos of them naked, having sex. Meanwhile, you had an intense desire to fund your charity. You also had some killer information regarding Ethan's phony birth certificate.

"You used your body to fund your charity, and they agreed to help because they wanted Mitch punished, or dead."

"You have a vivid imagination, Dani," she says. "I've always admired you for that."

"And I admire how you put all this together. I'm not upset over what you did to Ethan. The kid's a slime. The video proved it. He deserved to take a hit to his piggybank. Yes, you set him up, just like I do with my decoy work. But no one forced him to touch you. And you did ask him to stop. And he didn't."

"You wouldn't rather see him in jail? See justice done?"

"Justice *was* done. This is how you beat people like Ethan and Gavin. You take away their power, and their money. They'll get it back in other ways, but at least you come out ahead, and the kids you'll help through your charity."

"Thanks Dani. I really appreciate that."

"What about the job? Wouldn't it be fun for you, Kelli, and Parker to work with me someday?"

"I honestly don't see that in our futures, although you might be interested to know Parker and Kelli have changed their majors to Nonprofit Management and Social Entrepreneurship, respectively."

"So you *did* offer them jobs!"

"That's all I'm going to say."

"You'll miss the rush, you know."

"You think?"

"I would," I say.

"We'll stay busy. If we do our jobs right, we could change the world."

"You make it sound so much more noble than getting all dressed up to catch cheating husbands."

"We all serve in our own way," she says.

"Are you sure you're seventeen?"

She smiles. "I'm going to miss your flattery."

"I picked out a name for us," I say. "I was going to get matching t-shirts."

"Tell me."

"Brace yourself."

"Okay."

"*Dani's Decoys!*"

She smiles. "You'll have to carry on without us. I'm sure we'd have fun, but our donors would never approve. Nevertheless, if you *do* make the shirts, we'll wear them proudly."

With that, she gives me a big hug, removes the wedge from the door, places it on the counter, and walks out.

Epilogue

I don't blame Riley for not taking me up on my job offer. Being a decoy is far less prestigious than being the administrator of a major charity. Not to mention she can immediately start paying herself a substantial salary and fund all sorts of humanitarian projects. Like Gavin said, there are lots of organizations, including private schools, who'll provide matching funds for contributions up to a certain amount. When she makes Gavin's contribution public, it will be an irresistible story. It'll open the floodgates, and donor money will fly through the door. She'll get national exposure for it, and I'm not talking about the photos that have already been purged from the internet. Riley knows a multi-million dollar charity, properly administered, can generate a lifetime of income for her, while allowing her to do good deeds.

I'm not thrilled about my handling of what Dillon calls our pro-porno case. We did some things I'm not proud of, including breaking and entering, theft, and of course, I lied about watching the video, which I have since destroyed. I will say this was a very unique case, and I was emotionally vested in it. Still, I'm very, very sorry for the lies I told, the mistakes I made, and the laws I broke, or caused to be broken. I solemnly promise I won't break any laws from here on out, now, and forever more.

Of course, I made that very same promise after finishing my last case, too...

THE END

Call Me!

Dani Ripper and John Locke

Chapter 1

THURSDAY

"IT'S HARD TO look dignified with a dick in your mouth."

"*Excuse* me?"

My new client, Carter Teague, needs to understand I'm a decoy, not a hooker. In other words, I'm not going to have sex with her boyfriend.

"Fiancé," she says.

"Whatever. I'll get him in my hotel room, and you can walk in on us from the adjoining room. But we won't actually be naked."

Carter looks exasperated. "He could come up with a million excuses if you're dressed. But if I walk in and you're both naked, what's he going to say?"

She looks around my office.

I know what that means.

She's noting the disarray. The fact I don't have a secretary. And do have a bag of trash that's overdue for the garbage.

1

She checks my business card for the second time and sees my name, Dani Ripper, is not raised or embossed. She rightfully assumes a female private eye in Cincinnati, Ohio, rarely gets the big clients.

She knows I need the money.

"What if I sweeten the pot?" she says.

"I'm not a hooker, Ms. Teague."

"No, of course not!" Carter says, shaking her head. "I'm sorry. I didn't mean to imply—"

I wave her off. "It's okay. I just want to be clear."

There are two faux leather chairs across from my desk. Carter's sitting in the one closest to the door. She's thirty. Dressing younger, but thirty, which makes her six years older than me.

I'd stake my life on it.

Her shoulder-length hair is russet, with amber highlights, if you care about such things. I do, and make a note to ask who does her hair, though it's probably a week's pay for me. I did happen to notice her Casadei back-zip wedge sandals when she entered, though they're currently hidden by the desk. The part of her I *can* see is wearing an off-shoulder leopard tunic, with bracelets that match my annual house payment. She exudes wealth, and proves it by saying, "I'll pay you two thousand plus expenses."

"For two thousand you could hire the best hooker in town."

"This isn't about sex, Ms. Ripper. I don't want to catch him *cheating*, I just need to know if he *would*. There's a lot at stake here. The wedding *alone* will cost my father a quarter million."

Two grand means I get to keep driving my car.

"Bra and panties?" I offer.

"Three thousand," she says. "All cash."

"In advance?"

"If you wish."

I wince, thinking about it.

"Maybe I could lose the bra. But my panties aren't negotiable."

"Five thousand dollars!" she calls out with all the enthusiasm of a trophy wife at a charity auction. "All cash. In advance." She pauses, then says, "My final offer."

I bite my lip.

"Take it or leave it," she says.

"No photos," I say.

"*What?* Why not?"

"Are you *serious?*"

Carter sighs. "Deal."

Her fiancé's name is Joe Fagin. He's thirty-two. We review his photos together. She wants to set it up for tomorrow night at the Brundage Hotel in Louisville, where he has dinner reservations at Simon Claire's at seven-fifteen.

"Have you ever been there?" I ask.

"No."

"The restaurant's on the second floor. There's an open area, then the bar."

"Perfect."

"Who's Joe meeting for dinner?"

"Computer geeks, trying to raise money."

"Joe's a venture capitalist?"

"He thinks so, but my father suspects he can't fund his deals. Mind you, there's no evidence of that."

"Do you know if they have plans for after dinner?"

"Joe Fagin hanging out with computer geeks?" she laughs. "He's not the type. You'll see. I expect he'll lose them after dinner, probably hit the Brundage bar."

"Or catch a cab somewhere more exciting."

She frowns. "That could mess things up."

"I'll work it out."

"I admire your confidence."

"I'm confident I can get his attention. Enticing him to come to my room is something entirely different."

"You'll try your best?"

"Of course. But if he doesn't take the bait..."

"Then we live happily ever after."

"You'd consider him faithful if I can't seduce him in a single encounter?"

"Absolutely." She notes my puzzled expression and says, "I mean, *look* at you!"

I can't look at me, but she does. In fact, she studies me so deliberately it makes me uncomfortable.

She says, "If he can resist *you*, I'll marry him. If not, I'll be heartbroken, but better off."

She opens her purse and removes a bundle of hundreds wrapped in a Union City Bank paper band.

"That's five," she says.

To her amusement, I spread the bills across my desktop and run a counterfeit money pen over them. When I'm satisfied they're real, she reaches in her purse and removes another bundle of equal size and denomination, and peels five bills from that one.

"Expenses," she says.

I run the pen over those, as well.

As I watch her leave my office, I recall how she entered it thirty minutes earlier. She knocked on my door, tentatively. I told her to come in. When she did, she looked at me and her eyes widened.

That was the first thing I noticed, her eyes. I'd never seen harlequin-green eyes before.

"Wow," she said.

"Wow?"

"You're beautiful."

"Thanks," I said. "That's quite a compliment, coming from you."

And it was, because Carter Teague's a knockout. As a woman, I'm allowed to say that. I'm allowed to notice, too. It's funny how we can get away with looking at, and even touching, other women. I wasn't interested in touching her boobs, of course, but I could've said something like, "Are those real? No? Oh, my God, they're *spectacular!* May I?" Then I could've reached out and touched them. She would've been embarrassed, but she'd have allowed it. If a man tried that, he'd find himself in an orange jumpsuit before the noon whistle signals lunch at county.

Funny, that.

I think she caught me looking at her boobs just then, because she suddenly averted her eyes and pretended to glance out my office window. She did that a few seconds, then turned back and focused her eyes on mine.

"You're Ms. Ripper?" she said.

"Please. Call me Dani. And you're?"

"Carter Teague."

"Great name," I said.

"Thanks."

We were both quiet a moment.

"Um...you're staring," I said.

"Oh. Sorry!"

"No problem. I'm flattered. I think."

She wasn't blushing, more like flushed. And staring again.

"You're married?" she said.

"Yes."

"Happily?"

How does any married woman answer that question? Depends on the hour, the day, the time of month...

"I like to think so," I say. "How can I help you?"

She removed my business card from the card holder on my desk and held it between her perfectly manicured thumb and index finger.

"You're a private investigator?" she said.

"I am."

"I was told you're a decoy."

"By whom?"

"I heard my father talking to someone. He's a divorce attorney."

"Here?"

"No. Cleveland."

"And he's heard of *me*?"

"He was telling someone you're the best in the business."

"I've done some decoy work. Not locally."

"This would be in Louisville, not Cincinnati."

I nodded. She explained what she wanted, and how she planned to walk in on her fiancé and me while having sex, and

I explained how I don't actually have sex with the husbands or boyfriends, and—wait. I'm wasting your time. You're caught up. Let's move along.

Chapter 2

TWO THINGS HAVE happened. Carter Teague has left the building, and I've got another decoy job.

The sign on the door says *Dani Ripper, Private Investigator*. As does the ad in the phone book. The business cards. The social media listings all over the internet.

Dani Ripper, Private Investigator.

The word "decoy" cannot be found associated with my name, but that's the work I get.

I'm not shocked, there are reasons I'm not on the short list for the big PI jobs. First, I'm a woman.

I don't mean it the way you think.

What I mean is most clients think this type of work involves physical encounters with seamy, bent-nosed characters. Clients are conditioned to expect a PI who'll hang a brute on a meat hook and beat the shit out of him with a tire iron to find out where he hid the jewels. They tend to view me as tight jeans, five-inch heels, and a kick-ass halter.

I'm the first to admit I'm not tough.

I don't grunt, sweat, or smell. I know some basic moves, but I'm more at home on a dance floor than a kick boxing ring. In short, I don't look the part. Which is funny, since ninety-nine percent of the job involves computer and camera work, and sitting in cars waiting for people to exit homes, hotels or businesses. Less than one percent involves physical contact.

The second reason I don't get much PI business is I've never had a high-profile case. In this business one high profile case will feed you a lifetime of clients.

Let me amend that statement: I *have* had a high-profile case. I just didn't solve it. And that's the third reason I don't get much PI business.

I scoop Carter's cash off my desk and stuff it in my shoulder tote. I'm a Choo girl on a Kors budget, which is to say I'll splurge to a point when I get a windfall.

Which isn't often.

Today's a windfall, but I've already earmarked Carter's cash for practical things, like catching up on my car payments. And the mortgage. I'll also put a grand toward my step-son's college fund. Buy some groceries and household cleaning supplies. And...wait. I might have enough left to splurge. Tomorrow I'll buy a nice gift for best friend Sophie Alexander, whose birthday happens to be today. This morning Sophie was the proud recipient of a whimsical email card and an invitation to a birthday lunch on Tuesday. Thanks to Carter Teague, Sophie's lunch has been upgraded to dinner and a bracelet. I'll get her something trendy, but tasteful.

So the clothes, jewelry, fancy cars, mansions, yachts and such will be placed on hold till I finally crack a high-profile case. And that's fine, since I suspect it's more fun to dream about exquisite material things than it is to insure and maintain them. While I admit to owning a few signature pieces, like my Gucci watch (a gift from Sophie) I'm not a clothes whore. I'd much rather have a fond vacation memory than a pair of designer pumps.

With ninety minutes to kill before my lunch appointment with Vicky Stringfellow, I go back to what I was doing before Carter showered me with cash, which happens to be the same thing I always do when I have time on my hands.

Check my emails.

It's not what you think.

I check emails the same way you do, and read and answer them the same way you do. But, unlike you, I'm checking to see if my alerts have been triggered. I use all the alert programs, seeking hits to variations on the phrase that haunts my days and nights.

A quick scan shows no recent hits. But most of my alerts are updated every twenty-four hours, so I go to Google and type the word *cherrystones*.

167,000 entries.

I scan the first dozen pages, as always, but can't find what I want. I narrow the search by typing *Are your nipples like cherrystones?*

That phrase turns up 19,200 entries, but none on the first dozen pages contain the exact wording. So I try *nipples like cherrystones*.

And get 11,100,000 entries.

Crazy, right?

But as I scan the first dozen pages of this search, I find two references. One on a dating site, another in a chat room.

The dating site would be an uncharacteristic departure for my target, but my pulse quickens, as it always does, whenever these (or similar) words are typed in a chat room that underage girls are likely to frequent. I copy the link into my browser, click it, and learn it requires an annual credit card payment of nineteen dollars.

I sigh.

That brings my total to fourteen paid sites and forty-seven free ones. That's sixty-one sites if my math skills haven't deserted me. I check each of these sites at least once a week. Do I have that much time to spare?

No. But what am I going to do?

I'm obsessed.

I create a new email account and sign up with a unique name and password, and record the information in my notebook. Most chat room sites are so simple to navigate it only takes a minute to catch the groove, and this one's no different.

The boy/man/pervert? who made the reference is listed as *SeanInPain*, and his current status is *Offline*. There's no photo, but his avatar—consisting of the words *Bad Boy* scrawled in black ink with red blood dripping down the letters—is twisted enough to attract the twelve to fifteen-year-old female demographic my target seeks: those who think they want a brooding, dangerous, slightly-older guy.

I click his profile and roll my eyes. He claims to be from *Everywhere*. His age is described as *Old Soul*. His likes are *Let's just say you couldn't handle it!* His dislikes are *Whiny girls who run to mommy.*

A cold chill runs through my body. *SeanInPain* is a prime candidate!

I scroll his recent posts till I find the reference, written nineteen hours ago: *I saw my sister naked in the shower just now. Her breasts are small, the exact size of the silicone inserts I found in her underwear drawer last week. On the box they claim to increase your bra size by 1.5 cups. But if you lay them on a table, they're pretty damn flat. Sorry guys. My sister's tits are flat and unattractive. But her nipples are hard, like cherrystones. More on this soon.*

Asshole.

Not because he sneaks in the bathroom to spy on his sister, and not because he reports her nudity to the world. Sure, spying on your sister is over-the-top creepy, and this little shit has obviously got twenty-to-life issues.

But that's not what makes him an asshole.

What makes him an asshole is he cost me nineteen bucks and he's not the guy. *SeanInPain* is someone else's pervert. He's my guy ten years ago. But my pervert is older. Late twenties, I think. Used to call himself *ManChild.* When he writes the phrase in a chat room, it won't be an eye-witness report on his sister's cleavage. It'll be a question, asked by a grown man to a teenage girl between the ages of twelve and fifteen. And what he'll ask is, *Are your nipples like cherrystones? Are they hard and firm? Are they as hard and firm as the erection in my pants?*

There's more, of course, but I'll spare you the details. Just thinking about it makes me want to take a shower.

Chapter 3

VICKY STRINGFELLOW AND I greet each other the way we've been socially conditioned to greet other women: by raising our voices an octave, gushing with fake enthusiasm, and finding something about the other to compliment. She chooses my figure, I choose her eyes. Since I called the meeting, social etiquette requires me to throw in an extra compliment, so I say, "Vicky, where on earth did you find that killer top?"

She smiles. "You really like it?"

"I *love* it!"

"Believe it or not, I found it at Leversons."

We chitchat about where Leversons is located, and who I should ask for when I check it out. As we talk, we appraise each other the way we've been conditioned all our lives to appraise other women: by noting their flaws.

I'm well aware of mine, but if you want that information you'll have to ask Vicky. As for hers, I'm not overly critical, and I want very much to like her, so I'll just say she's a little overweight, and could use some help with hair and makeup. On the other hand, she's intelligent, pleasant, and available.

"How long have you been divorced?" I say.

I didn't just blurt that out, we're actually twenty minutes into the conversation at this point, and the waiter has just brought our salads, and fussed over us with offers of fresh-ground pepper and hand-grated cheese.

Vicky tells me what I need to know about her and Charles: they broke up two years ago, no kids, she teaches fourth grade at a private school, and has her own townhome in Willoughby Commons. She's dated several men, but nothing clicked because she wasn't ready to begin a new relationship.

Till now.

As she talks, I mentally tick each item with a checkmark on my list. Vicky's not bitter or needy. She's independent, self-sustaining, and ready to move on with her life.

"So..." she says, and I know we've come to the tricky part.

"Yes?"

"Tell me about this professor you've found for me."

"He teaches at Clifton State."

She arches her eyebrows. In a good way. But waits for me to continue.

"His name's Ben Davis," I say. "He's thirty-eight."

She lifts her chin slightly, purses her lips. I know what she's thinking.

Vicky Davis.

Her eyes widen the slightest bit. I wouldn't have noticed had I not been studying her so closely. But her eyes tell me Vicky likes the sound of her name with Ben's, a critical issue, since she's still using her married name.

"How long have you known Ben?" she asks.

"Seven years."

"And you *still* think he's a good guy?"

She laughs.

I laugh.

"He's a *great* guy," I say. "A true gentleman. The smartest man I know."

She frowns. "If he's that great, why aren't *you* dating him?"

I bite my bottom lip. "I'm married."

She instinctively looks at my left hand.

"You're not wearing a ring."

"It's complicated."

Vicky nods, slowly. She wants to pursue the conversation, but doesn't want to intrude, or appear too nosey this early in our relationship. Steering the conversation back to Ben, she says, "How many times has the good professor been married?"

"Twice."

"Oh," she says, suddenly deflated. She frowns.

"It's not as bad as it sounds," I say.

"Tell me why."

"Well, he's only been divorced once."

She cocks her head. "One of his wives passed away?"

My turn to frown. I have to word this carefully. This is the part where I always lose them. I rehearsed it in my head ten times, but it should have been twenty, because the right words aren't coming.

Vicky says, "Did one of his wives die?"

"Not exactly."

She frowns again. At the pace she's frowning, I wonder how long it'll take her face to develop worry lines.

"I'm afraid I don't understand," Vicky says. "He's been married twice, divorced once, and one of his wives hasn't passed away. Is this a riddle?"

"It *can* be."

"Excuse me?"

"Here's the thing. He's still married."

"*What?*" She jumps to her feet.

"Wait. It's not what you think. Please. Sit down."

She frowns again. Vicky's quite angry, but we're in a public place and people are staring at us. Common courtesy dictates she at least offer to split the check. She knows this, and starts fumbling around in her purse.

"Vicky," I say, "please. Let me explain."

She sighs, and reclaims her seat.

"I don't appreciate your wasting my time like this," she says. "You can't possibly think I'd be interested in dating a married man."

I hold up my hand. "Ordinarily I wouldn't. But this guy's special. You can get to know him on Mondays and Tuesdays."

"He's *married*, Dani. That's a deal-breaker."

"Here's the thing," I say.

"Yes?"

"He's married to me."

"*What?*"

"Ben's my husband. And I swear, he's a wonderful man."

She looks around. "Are there cameras in here? Am I being punked?"

"No, of course not."

"Then...what? Are you insane?"

"Not clinically. I don't think. Well, maybe."

Vicky places a twenty on the table by her untouched salad. "This should more than cover my lunch," she says. She stands, walks about twenty feet, turns, and comes back to the table.

"Does Ben know you're shopping him around?"

"No. It would kill him if he found out."

Her eyes become slits. "Are you telling me he doesn't even know you're planning to leave him?"

I look down at my salad.

She says, "How long have you been cheating on him?"

I say nothing, though I've never cheated on Ben.

"When are you planning to tell him?"

"I won't leave him till I know he's got a better woman than me in his life."

She frowns for a record fifth time. "No offense," she says, "but I don't think it'll take much of a woman to be an improvement."

I flash a hopeful smile. "Does that mean you're willing to meet him?"

She spins around and starts walking away, swiftly.

I holler, "We could have you over for dinner!"

Personal Message from John Locke:

If you like my books, you'll LOVE my mailing list! By joining, you'll receive discounts of up to 67% on future eBooks. Plus, you'll be eligible for amazing contests, drawings, and you'll receive immediate notice when my newest books become available!
Visit my website:
http://www.DonovanCreed.com

John Locke

New York Times Best Selling Author

8th Member of the Kindle Million Sales Club
(which includes James Patterson, Stieg Larsson,
George R.R. Martin and Lee Child, among others)

John Locke had 4 of the top 10 eBooks on
Amazon/Kindle at the same time, including #1 and #2!

...Had 6 of the top 20, and 8 books in the top 43 at the same time!

...Has written 19 books in three years in
four separate genres, all best-sellers!

...Has been published in numerous languages by many of
the world's most prestigious publishing houses!

John Locke

New York Times Best Selling Author
#1 Best Selling Author on Amazon Kindle

Donovan Creed Series:
Lethal People
Lethal Experiment
Saving Rachel
Now & Then
Wish List
A Girl Like You
Vegas Moon
The Love You Crave
Maybe
Callie's Last Dance

Emmett Love Series:
Follow the Stone
Don't Poke the Bear
Emmett & Gentry
Goodbye, Enorma

Dani Ripper Series:
Call Me!
Promise You Won't Tell?

Dr. Gideon Box Series:
Bad Doctor
Box

Other:
Kill Jill

Non-Fiction:
How I Sold 1 Million eBooks in 5 Months!

Made in the USA
Lexington, KY
20 July 2015